George Washington Hosmer

As we Went Marching on

George Washington Hosmer

As we Went Marching on

ISBN/EAN: 9783744711661

Printed in Europe, USA, Canada, Australia, Japan

Cover: Foto ©Andreas Hilbeck / pixelio.de

More available books at **www.hansebooks.com**

"AS WE WENT MARCHING ON"

A Story of the War

By G. W. HOSMER, M.D.

NEW YORK
HARPER & BROTHERS, FRANKLIN SQUARE
1885

"AS WE WENT MARCHING ON."

CHAPTER I.

ON THE PICKET-LINE.

ACROSS our front, and not very far away, ran a road that led from Culpepper on the south toward Lost Mountain and Ashby's Gap on the north; and the Colonel passed some time every night on that road. One glorious, silent, starlight night he explored it as usual, accompanied only by Captain Pembroke, who was then acting as major—for the major had been killed at Malvern Hills. They had ridden with customary care a mile, perhaps, beyond our last picket, and toward the south, when the Colonel heard a sound ahead which he stopped to consider. He was soon satisfied there was a horseman coming down this road toward them. He heard clearly in a few moments the jingle of accoutrements, and then a voice singing the Southern doggerel, "Hurrah for the bonnie blue flag, that bears a single star." It was a Confederate soldier, therefore; but were there more behind him? Was it a case that required a rapid ride to our lines that the men might be put under arms to be ready for any possibility, or was this merely some straggler unaware that there were Union troops near by? Or was this horseman, indeed, the bait to a trap?

Dave had often laughed at the simplicity of certain of our newly-fledged regimental and brigade commanders, who had only come down South to be caught in some easy trap and be marched away prisoners by Mosby or others of that kidney. Indeed for mishaps of that sort there was no sympathy, and the old man knew it would never do to be caught in that way.

And yet if he should ride away from this possible trap and give an alarm in camp!

An old soldier does not put his men under arms after taps for slight reasons, and never on suspicion. Hasty and inconsiderate alarms are common where soldiers are new to their duty; but they did not occur in old Dave's camp. In the few moments before the stranger came into view over the hill in front, the Colonel judged that it would be safe to see clearly what was behind this night-rambler, and then if he was alone they would take him; for a prisoner is an article of value in all cases where information in regard to the movements of the enemy is so scarce as it was with us at that period. He may not mean to tell you anything, but he cannot help it. The mere name of his regiment or division tells what troops are near you.

And a soldier is always proud to tell the name of

his commander, because he glories in the achieve-
ments of his own corps. Between Manassas and
Gainesville, in that very campaign, one of our companies got a fellow who wouldn't say a word—held
his mouth as tight as a bear-trap. But when he was
asked, with an indifferent air, what army he was in,
he lifted up his head and said, " General Longstreet's, sir." Well, that fact was of wonderful consequence to us. It had been supposed that we were
on Stonewall Jackson's flank, and that he was cut
off ; but here was Longstreet in front. That fellow
saved our army from wasting five thousand men in
a vain battle: yet his fixed purpose was not to give
any information.

Dave, who knew all the value of a prisoner, consequently led Pembroke into the shadow of the
woods, and they waited for the stranger, who came
in sight in a very little while.

He was a handsome figure in the starlight. He
sat with an easy and gallant air a tall bay, whose fine
limbs they saw would bother them greatly if she
had a chance to run for her rider's liberty, and
whose restiveness showed that an easy gait was taken
for some other reason than consideration for her.

Confederate soldiers whose uniforms could be
fairly called fresh or brilliant were seldom seen on
our front at any place or time; for they were not
put near, apparently, till the tough experiences of a
soldier's life had dimmed the bravery of the first
suit, and a second suit was an unknown fact. But
this soldier's suit was less dingy than common. His

gray seemed to have a gloss of newness; and his
buttons and gold lace and other frippery, though
their glitter was perhaps exaggerated by the deceptive illumination of the stars, seemed to declare
themselves ignorant of the vicissitudes of a campaign.

Dave consequently indulged doubts whether this
could be one of Lee's men. If he was, he had
joined Lee's army lately, and the army was not far
away; for this fellow seemed to come out of a
bandbox. Yet there was about him so much of the
style of an old soldier he could not be a mere recruit.
Altogether, there was enough in the circumstance
to mystify our two friends hidden in the shadow of
the wood by the roadside; but this puzzle did not
distract their thoughts from the principal doubt of
the moment. Was he alone? They soon felt sure
that he was, for the road was clear for several hundred yards behind him, and no sound came from
that direction.

But deliberation was soon cut short, for just as
the stranger came opposite our hidden friends his
keen nag turned her nose almost as if she were a
pointer to Dave and Pembroke in the shadow, and
she gave an energetic snort, and Pembroke's horse
whinnied an answer; whereupon the stranger drew
up suddenly, and scanned for a second that point
of animated gloom by the wayside; but before he
had resolved the doubts in his mind, or determined
a line of action, Dave gave the word, and the two
charged together, and with cocked pistols held

against his head at either side almost before he knew it, he had no discretion. To surrender was the only possible course for a rational creature.

The prisoner now rode into our lines between his captors. His light-heartedness was gone; and that buoyant gayety which had found vent in the popular refrain was replaced by a despondency so sudden and deep as to seem to old Dave almost unmanly. He thought the natural fortitude or bravado of a youngster—even if not reinforced by the defiant spirit of an enemy—should enable one to face an always imminent mischance with more resolution than appeared in the prisoner. Dave thought it natural that a soldier should be in the dumps in such circumstances; but to be so terribly down as this fellow was seemed to him to imply some more than ordinary apprehension: and from that to the notion that it was necessary to know particularly all about this prisoner was not far.

"Why," said Dave, "if you had been taken as a spy inside our lines, and were to be hanged in half an hour, you could not be more broken up."

"If it were only facing death for myself," said the reb, quietly, "I am too familiar with that experience to heed it a great deal."

"Ah! then there is more in the case than your life or death?"

"Yes, sir."

"Your capture concerns the welfare of others?"

"Yes, sir; at least of another."

Dave's mystification was only made deeper. Was

this fellow really a spy, thus surprised into a half-confession, and regarding his own fate as trivial in comparison with the consequences his capture would produce for his brigade or division? And what did "another" mean? Had he an accomplice?

Old Dave, Pembroke, and the prisoner went into the old man's tent, and the captive was called upon to give an account of himself. The story he told was so simple and covered the case so completely that the old man was hardly satisfied with it, for his suspicions once awakened were not easily lulled.

The prisoner's name was Arthur Willoughby, his home was near Front Royal, and he was a soldier in the rebel Army of Northern Virginia. In the battle of the Seven Pines he had been engaged with his regiment in the attempt to drive our fellows down the Williamsburg road; but in that action he had been wounded and taken to Richmond. There he had been prostrated through the whole of June and part of July; had finally got on foot, but was yet unfit for duty; and as Richmond was crowded with men wounded in the later battles, he had started for his home, in the hope to recuperate there, and had stopped for some days, almost exhausted, at Orange Court-house.

He knew nothing whatever of the immediate movements of the Confederate forces.

Old Dave did not believe this story, and he said severely:

"Do you mean to tell me, sir, that you, a soldier, riding at night a good nag such as yours, and within maybe ten or twenty miles of the advance of Lee's army, have not had the curiosity to inquire as to the whereabouts of even your own regiment?"

"Sir," said the prisoner with quiet dignity, "since you do not believe me, my own repeated declaration of the same fact will not convince you; but reason on the case from your own stand-point. You are as near to Lee's army as I am. You have perhaps been endeavoring for some time to ascertain its exact whereabouts. From what you say I judge that you do not know much about it. If with all your efforts you have not acquired this knowledge, how should I possess it, having made no endeavor to gain it?"

"But what I do not understand," said Dave, "is that you should have made no such endeavor."

"On that side perhaps I am to blame," said the other. "Some preoccupation of mind that I may call domestic has too much withdrawn my thoughts from my patriotic duties."

As we soon knew, the preoccupation thus referred to was the real point in the case; and what it involved made friends for the prisoner in our camp. But the Colonel got no more out of him that night.

All this happened, as I said, on the road that ran across our front, and which was a few hundred yards beyond our picket-line. Our battalion was posted at that time far out in the valley beyond Thoroughfare Gap; and it was in August, 1862, when the common trouble was for a time that everybody was posted in the wrong place.

From the Westover plantation on the James River, from that great fair field of grain which was so beautiful when we marched into it on the day after Malvern Hills, and which so soon became an almost bottomless slough of mud,—and a slough of despond it seemed for our army,—from the *ennui*, and the fever, and the heat of an almost tropical summer, the boys had been brought up, a brigade and a division at a time; and from the Bull Run mountains to Washington the State of Virginia was pretty well peppered with them, except as to points where pepper was needed; for, in the eyes of some one who did not know us, it had been deemed wiser to send the army by instalments to a new commander than to send a new commander to the army.

How it happened that our regiment had been sent to that point out in the valley none of us ever knew. Our division was not in that neighborhood; neither, so far as I know, was any other part of the Army of the Potomac. But it occurred often enough in our experience that when a regiment was wanted for an emergency of any sort,—often also only an imagined emergency,—the nearest regiment to the officer who imagined the emergency was caught up and sent off at race-horse speed without any consideration of the way in which that practice disorganized good divisions and brigades. So we always supposed that we must have been some day or night too near to a general possessed of more authority than he knew how to use, and that this day had been one of those critical ones when the movements of two Union armies made a military phantasmagoria in that part of Virginia; when Lee's army was "lost," and when the prevalent theory of the military authorities was that Lee was heading for the Shenandoah Valley by way of Luray and Front Royal. Our duty had regard apparently to the possibilities of that theory of the enemy's operations.

But, however it came about that we were sent there, there we were.

Old Dave, the Colonel, swore freely, eloquently, and picturesquely on that occasion, as indeed he did on nearly all occasions. His most memorable achievement in that way was when General Benham, the engineer, gave orders which required him to put his regiment across a pontoon-bridge near Fredericksburg left in front. He swore then with an intense and loyal respect for tactics and the honor of a soldier which would have gained for him, had it been generally known, the enthusiastic admiration of the army. On this occasion he was less energetic, but his style always had freshness and vigor in it.

No chronicler can safely declare where Dave acquired this habit which so often procures for a soldier his only satisfaction. It may have been at West Point, though that is hardly probable. More likely it was on the plains; and yet there could not have been a great deal to swear at there, for in the days of Dave's service the Indians always had the worst

of it.   There was no doubt the usual proportion of
bad weather in that region, and the common share of
disappointments due to the delay of rations, mails,
and other comforts; but these are things that rather
give occasion for the exercise of the habit once
formed than lead to its original formation.

Perhaps it was the old man's instinctive perception of a necessary element in military life.   Old
soldiers have always sworn ; and what has happened
for thousands of years in the same occupation must
have some necessary relation to its moral moods.
How the army swore in Flanders everybody knows.
Soldiers cannot make peevish complaint ; and they
cannot run away.   They must stand and face the
" cussedness of things " in whatever form it comes ;
their only resource is to open fire.   And whether
they open with a field-piece, or with a sulphurous
vocabulary, the satisfaction is the same in kind.

Despite his constant objurgations on the subject, an
isolated position was one that suited very well the taste
of the Colonel ; for he rather preferred to live on the
picket-line, and was certainly to be found at some
point of it at any hour when there was a possibility
of a call from the enemy.   He always explored personally every doubtful locality near his lines inside
and out, and every individual picket was posted on
tactical and even strategic reasons, so that there
should be the least likelihood of his being found at
a disadvantage in a critical moment.

Dave was engaged in that way when Willoughby
was taken.   Willoughby, as hinted, soon made

friends in the regiment, and the truthful spirit of his reflections upon the war helped in that respect. One of the things that convinced us he always told the truth was the circumstance that he recollected a piece of history which, unconsciously to him, was very agreeable to our vanity. His account of the Seven Pines battle was that the advance of the division he was in was arrested and the tide of battle stayed by the resistance of a regiment which held a rail-fence on the ground immediately north of the York River Railroad. Now, that rail-fence north of the railroad was held by our regiment, and we consequently conceived that this fellow's head was more than usually level.

But in his repeated histories of that rail-fence the prisoner was always disposed to consider the tenacity of resistance at that point as due to the cover which the fence supplied to the regiment behind it, until old Maltby said, in his dry, quaint, surly way:

"Yes, there's no doubt that rail-fence protected us—just as a gridiron protects a beefsteak from the fire."

Not much more was said about the fence.

At that time it was not convenient to send him to the rear, and consequently Willoughby was kept a close prisoner in a tent the first night and the next day, and a file of men was told off from the guard to watch him.

None knew at the moment, except the Colonel and Captain Pembroke, what account the prisoner had given of himself; but we all thought from the strict

way in which he was put under guard that his story
had not satisfied the Colonel; and there was much
speculation in regard to him. Who was he? What
was he? Was he only an ordinary prisoner? Had
he come over? Was he only a scout, and was this
mode of putting him under guard only played to
deceive possible spies of the enemy in our lines?
Was he, perhaps, a spy himself? Opinions and
theories of this sort were commonly indulged on
such an occasion.

Our prisoner was regarded, in short, with that
sentiment of curious interest which always centres
about any person who is believed to stand in some
critical or perilous position, or to be passing some
crisis of his fate.

If Willoughby cared to conceal from ordinary
observers that chagrin, apprehension, or despair—
whatever it was—that made him so cast down when
he was first brought into camp, his close confinement
could scarcely have been disagreeable to him; but
he was, as we subsequently knew, a person who
would have preferred it the other way, and who
cared more for sympathy than for his dignity. Indeed, he did not feel that it was against his dignity
to be an object of commiseration.

CHAPTER II.

THE PRISONER AND HIS STORY.

TOWARD nightfall the next day, the Colonel, reassured by the tranquillity about us as to any possible connection between the prisoner and a move of the enemy, decided that it was unnecessary to keep the young fellow under guard any longer; so he was put upon his parole not to escape, and given his liberty from immediate restraint; and Captain Pembroke invited him to make himself at home in his mess.

From that time we saw him almost as much as we saw Pembroke himself, for they were a great deal together.

Willoughby was tall and well made, with the graceful, easy air of a well-bred man; but withal somewhat boyish in his open demeanor, and in the readiness with which he gave his confidence to any one who came near. In his appearance he was a Virginian out and out, for he was sallow rather than bronzed by exposure; bony rather than muscular; and his hair was worn longer than in the North we are used to seeing men's hair—a sort of affectation caught up, it seems, by Virginians from the traditions of the style of the Cavaliers; an artistic notion, perhaps, of contrasting an effeminate appearance with the reality of manly qualities.

He was a light-hearted fellow, and he came out from his gloom under the influence of good company. He did not recover himself entirely; but the gloom came upon him only by fits and starts. He would be gay, good-humored, and apparently as happy as any one, taking an amused interest in whatever was going on; but any occasion of tranquillity or loneliness that threw him upon his remembrances for occupation revived again all the poignancy of his chagrin.

Between him and Pembroke there were similarities and differences equally notable. Pembroke was a man of about the same height as Willoughby,—and each was a little short of six feet,—but the Captain had the more robust air, though he was probably not really any larger than the other. His air did not belie him, in fact, for he was a man of almost marvellous physical endurance. He had clear blue eyes; a skin naturally rather fair, but bronzed almost to the color of an Indian by the exposures of campaigning; and his brown hair was cut short. He was the most amiable and companionable man in the regiment—but also the most reticent.

Indeed he talked so little, and especially so little about himself, that we knew nothing of his family or history, and therefore we imagined there was some mystery in it.

Supper for his mess was spread that night on a cloth laid out in front of Pembroke's tent; and he, the doctor, the chaplain, and the prisoner ate together.

Although the Captain was always quiet, and Willoughby on this occasion diffident and shy, there was never any scarcity of conversation where the doctor and the chaplain were met in one place; for they were both talkative and fitted to draw one another out because of a chronic yet semi-playful antipathy that was always between them.

Willoughby was, as they sat down, just a trifle startled at catching sight of the form of the table upon which the cloth was spread; for of course, though the cloth hid the table, the shape showed through.

Now they spread their dishes on the top of the mess-chess: but then their mess-chest was a coffin. This may seem rather an odd appurtenance to be used in such a way, and may give a false impression of the character of the gentlemen in that mess, as making it appear that they indulged in a sort of braggart mockery in mere vanity of indifference as to things that might be unpleasant to others. But there was nothing like that in it; and if it showed character at all, it only showed that like true soldiers they always made the best of circumstances and were ready to use what was useful without prejudice. To "take the goods the gods provide" is a good rule in view of the privations of war.

But the fact came about in a queer way, and resulted from the thrifty spirit of Norris, the private who was detailed to that mess.

He found this coffin on his hands one day. Somebody had sent it from the North as a proper receptacle for the body of an officer killed at Hanover

2

Court-house, and Norris had given it shelter till the body should be obtained. But the ground where the officer lay was within the enemy's lines, and the coffin seemed finally to be abandoned where it was left.

Norris carefully abstracted the white satin lining and gave it to a young woman in the neighborhood, who trimmed a new Sunday bonnet with it; and into the stout mahogany box thus left he packed his traps and stores. He found that when he had put his frying-pans and gridirons and dishes, and some sugar and spice and other commodities therein, they packed well and did not take up so much room as usual in the old ambulance-wagon in which such things were carried; while thus the coffin itself was practically out of the way, as it became a mere wrapper to necessary articles.

And in a spirit of true philosophy he said, "What is a coffin but a wrapper, anyhow?"

In fact the common name for those things in the army was "a wooden overcoat."

And then one day Norris's famous mess-chest developed an unexpected virtue which gave it an incalculable value in the eyes of that thrifty soldier. In the battle of the last day of May, 1862, our camp was lost by the failure of a regiment on our left to hold its position; and when it was retaken, it was by the advance of another division than ours. Thus the camp was for four or five hours in the hands of the enemy, and for about as long a time in the hands of some fellows on our side: and which gave the most attention to plundering I don't know; but when we had time to send some fellows there to try and get our property, it was a marvellously cleaned-out place.

Blankets, clothes, extra boots and shoes, slippers, clean shirts, writing-cases, precious black bottles, all the little comforts of camp-life were gone. But there was one thing there that the plunderers had treated with absolute respect: Norris's mess-kit was intact. They had seen its shining receptacle with the top well screwed down; they had concluded that the owner of it was inside, and at home, and they had left him alone in his glory.

Norris was a happy man, and he said, "Anybody would be a fool to abandon a mess-chest which by its shape alone can assure the safety of the things you put in it. It's better than one of those salamander iron safes, and nothing like so heavy."

So he rigged the cover with hinges, and they kept their coffin and used it for a table.

The chaplain caught the glance with which Willoughby took in this peculiar feature of the feast, and said:

"Yes, it's a queer shape, isn't it? Long and narrow, with odd protrusions at the sides, like the shoulder-angles of a bastion; but nobody ever complains that it isn't roomy."

"Somebody might complain," said Willoughby, "that it didn't improve his appetite."

"True enough," said the chaplain; "but it never affects us in that way. We are a little like the rats a farmer had up in Vermont."

" Pet rats ?"

" No ; opposition rats."

" What did they do ?"

" Well, they stole the farmer's cheese so persist-
ently that at last he had his cheese run into moulds
made the shape of cats."

"Because he thought cats handsome ?" said the
doctor.

" No ; because he thought it would bluff off the
rats."

" Did it ?"

" Why, the rats would eat a hole into one of those
cats and live there. They don't judge things by
superficial accidents ; and that's why I say we're
like 'em : we don't stop for trifles when it's feeding-
time."

And so they fell to.

" Did you hear, sir," said the doctor to Willoughby as there came an interval—" did you hear,
sir, before you left your lines, that the Northern
militia was in this part of the State ?"

" No, sir," said Willoughby, " I did not hear it."

" We received some new uniforms a little while
ago," said the doctor, "and we thought we should
be reported for militia."

"Mr. Farrington," said the chaplain to the doctor, " that is a dull sort of joke ; and it would be
polite to give the foe credit for more accurate perceptions."

" For my part," said Willoughby, with a very courteous delicacy, "having seen your battalion drawn

up at guard-mounting to-day, I do not believe that
any person with any military experience would ever
mistake your men for any other than well-seasoned,
veteran troops."

At this each one of the three instinctively lifted his
tin cup of spring-water tinctured with commissary
whiskey, and with a quiet inclination of the head
accepted the pleasant opinion as a personal favor.
With a happy tact Willoughby had reached the
hearts of all, and there was good-will among them.

So they warmed into an agreeable comradeship;
and by and by Willoughby, as he gathered that there
was some curiosity about him, volunteered information and told his story.

He named his regiment again, and spoke with a
pride which they appreciated of its qualities and
services, and told of the enthusiasm for freedom
with which he and all his comrades of the same
neighborhood had taken up arms.

"Only," said the chaplain, "and not to interrupt
you, we on our side though we hear it so often from
your side, can never get used to your theory that it
is 'for freedom' you fight, and can't comprehend
how you see it that way."

"Well, our opinions are naturally not the same
on that point," said Willoughby.

"Certainly, certainly," said the chaplain. "I only
mentioned it as a little difficulty your views give
us."

"Nobody in the world, I suppose," said the Captain, "can be absolutely sure that he is right on any

point whatever.   But everybody has his opinion
that he is right; and when he fights, the thing he
fights for is that opinion; and if he calls it the right
instead of his opinion of the right, he does only
what all men have always done."

"Well, I will accept that as a statement of my
position," said Willoughby.

"And when it has all to be summed up at the
last day, I imagine," continued the Captain, "the true
point will be, not which one of a thousand varying
views was right, but with how much honesty, courage,
and fidelity each man fought for that which he believed to be the right."

"That is a very correct and philosophical observation," said the doctor. "Now, then, for Mr. Willoughby's story."

"Well," said Willoughby, "before I went to the
army there had been in my life a delightful experience; and there was at that period a still more delightful vista for the future."

"Lady in the case?" said the chaplain.

"Yes, sir, that was it," said the Captain.

"Proves a man to have a healthy mind and to
be without a cynical spirit to find him in love," said
the doctor. "She is of course the most perfect of
her sex."

"Well, gentlemen," said Willoughby, "I can
hardly expect you to admit that, as you would naturally have some opinions and preferences of your
own on this theme also; but if your good fortune
had thrown you into the part of the country where

I was brought up, and you had been brought into relation with this lady as you were with the ladies whom you love or have loved, you would have loved her instead of these ladies."

At this they all roused up somewhat, and the doctor said:

"Very likely, very likely; but it's extremely lucky for you that it did not happen that way; since, for my part, though I am not a very handsome man, I am successful with the women, and I haven't the slightest doubt I should have cut you out."

"Now, then," said the chaplain, "let us all admit that she is the paragon of womankind, and that she would have loved the doctor,—and so get on with the story."

"Well, there is not much story beyond this," said Willoughby; "I loved this lady, and the passion was reciprocated. We were to be married, and in that delicious anticipation lived through the entranced days of the months before the war. But when the war came, the opinions of our friends were that that was not a time for marrying, and I went away with my regiment, leaving the lady at her home."

"Well, she will wait for you," said the Captain.

"Certainly," said Willoughby; "but is not waiting misery? She waited and waits. As I lay wounded lately at Orange Court-house, it was agreed between our families that since I was now not fit for active service and apparently would not be immediately, and as it was believed also that the war was perhaps over,—for they seem to have exaggerated the effect of General Lee's victories,—it was arranged on account of these things that I should go to her house and that we should be married now."

"And you were on the way the other night," said the chaplain.

"Just so. I should have been there by this time; and we would perhaps have been married to-morrow."

"Well, upon my word!" said the chaplain; "that was a misfortune."

And Willoughby was comforted by the evident and open sympathy of all.

"It is only deferred," said the Captain.

"True enough," said the other. "But if a thing chances to be deferred and deferred, people get a superstitious fancy that it is never to happen; and who can altogether free himself from such fancies? Besides, it is a time of uncertainty. Who knows what may happen from day to day? She may imagine that I am killed, or even that I have become indifferent."

"She will have faith if she is the woman she should be, and she will be constant," said the Captain; "and an old song declares that absence makes the heart grow fonder. On a point of that nature an old song should be a good authority. She will not love you the less for these mishaps."

"Why, I do not apprehend that she will," said Willoughby; "but who does not desire to be with the

woman he loves?. However tenderly he may be regarded in his absence, a man is always ready to
sacrifice that advantage for what he holds to be the
greater one of being with the lady."

Hereupon the doctor and the chaplain rambled
into an extravagant discussion as to whether a man
perfectly in love did ever leave the lady from the
conviction that she would love him more if he were
away than by her side; the doctor holding that that
might be the state of a woman's mind if the chaplain were the lover—and the chaplain maintaining
that if the doctor were the lover the woman would
necessarily love him so little either present or absent
that the difference would be imperceptible; and
meanwhile the Captain and Willoughby kept on a
quiet chat in interchange of such notions as presented themselves, when, the supper being over, they
filled and lighted the mutual pipe—an instrument
which the Indians did well to employ as an apparatus
for the ratification of treaties of peace.

They were two fine, handsome, generous fellows,
and friendship grew between them.

Friendship is an indulgence of the inclination of
two souls, and is an association without other object
than the indulgence of such an inclination; for
where a relation of two men has any other or more
material impulse, it is an interested alliance and
not a pure friendship. It seemed to me in view of
this standard that that was a pure friendship. They
would perhaps have been friends, meeting in any
circumstances. But their friendship assumed a ro-

mantic aspect due to the occasion ; for when natures thus adapted for sympathy are under uniforms of a different color, and the fact that they are foes by their cause though kindred souls by sentiment is ever before them, duty and friendship are equally put to severe tests.

Although the Colonel had found it difficult to believe Willoughby's story, it seemed reasonable enough to all the young fellows to whom Pembroke repeated it. Dave's incredulity was due to the fact that he gave all Southern men credit for more energy in their cause than they really possessed. Northern opinion at that time was that the South was far ahead of us in that respect: which was not true, at least not to the extreme to which it was believed.

But Dave, misled by that assumption, could not believe that this fellow could be on this errand with Lee on foot as he was ; youth and a fellow-feeling helped the rest of us to comprehend it.

CHAPTER III.

MARCHING AND FIGHTING.

WITHIN a few hours all was movement, activity, and rush in our camp.

Stonewall Jackson had slipped through the Bull Run mountains behind us; for as we were far enough out to keep our eyes on the Shenandoah Valley, we were too far to watch the route by which he came: and that, moreover, was not our duty. But when it was discovered that Longstreet was following Jackson on the same line, it was plain that we might be cut off, and our orders were to get through the gap in a hurry; orders which contemplated that we would then be in the same position with the whole army— between Jackson and Longstreet.

Our right company was on the road in an hour from the time we received these orders, and made twelve miles before it halted, for it was a pleasant part of the summer march; but we were not all together until somewhat later, for Pembroke, who had the left, was compelled to get everybody on the road ahead of him, and did not march himself until we were half way to our bivouac. The last news we received in that camp was that Pembroke had been promoted and was major.

Willoughby, on parole not to escape, marched with Pembroke.

Some fellows of the cavalry communicated with our pickets near daylight, and reported to the Colonel that the head of Longstreet's column was north of Orlean, and that if we did not get through Salem the next day we would find Longstreet in our way when we should reach that place. Consequently the old man had us out at peep of day in the hope to get through a good pull before the sun came upon us. None of the struggles of a soldier's life is harder than that struggle to get his eyes open and his head upright when he has not more than half slept out the night that follows a rapid march in the fine clear air.

But we did it then, as often in other times also; and we made a good march that day, though it was a hot and dusty one, and the men were a little inclined to straggle. It was not the fault of the marching, therefore, that when we came in the neighborhood of Salem, in the twilight, there was some doubt whether the horsemen we saw were our cavalry or the enemy's. We pushed on, however, with a line of flankers south of the place, and soon found out that the enemy was near; for two or three shots gave the alarm, and presently our fellows in that direction were popping away as fast as they could load and fire.

Perhaps some of us listened to our hopes rather than consulted our experience when we formed the opinion that our boys out on the flank were wrong, and that in the dim light they had mistaken our cavalry for that of the enemy.

But we soon got over that fancy, for in a few minutes we heard, far beyond the firing, the clear bugle-call "boots and saddles," and we knew it was the enemy's bugle. Evidently, therefore, our flankers to the south of our line of march were in collision with the enemy's cavalry-pickets; those pickets had reported us to their main body in the rear, and that main body was humping itself for a row.

Old Dave gave some rapid instructions to Pembroke, left him in command, and rode ahead in the direction of our line of march, evidently to see what sort of ground there was for a fight, and how we could be handled to the best advantage. In consequence of those orders we were formed up in open column, and marched that way until word came from the Colonel, when we were double-quicked in the same order to a position in an orchard, to reach which we went straight forward through a broken fence, for the road at that point obliqued to the right. As soon as we were halted we were deployed, and thus we were in line of battle in a jiffy, and all was done as handsomely as if on a dress-parade.

Our line was on very good ground, which sloped away in front so that the apple-trees below masked us; and as the road crossed our front only about a hundred yards away, there was an obstacle of broken fences that would hold the cavalry under our fire for a few minutes.

Our flankers, who now, in fact, formed a skirmish-line, had all they could do to get in when the rebel cavalry came with a burst. But we were ready for them, and gave them a blizzard that emptied about twenty saddles before they knew where the fire came from. They were astonished, perhaps, to find a whole battalion here, and went away; but there were plenty more behind them, and these were perhaps ordered to find out what this meant, for in a little while they came again stronger than before.

We gave them on that second occasion all that any reasonable cavalrymen could possibly want; for the boys, who had been dull at the tired end of the march, were now revived by this bit of fun, and fired with spirit. Besides, our ground was so well chosen—we had them so fairly before us at the road, and could hit them so well anywhere on the sweeping slope of the orchard—that we punished them tremendously without even the chance of getting a scratch ourselves.

Naturally the enemy got tired of that and seemed to give it up; and there was one of those lulls in which the only wonder with the boys is, What next?

Then there was a good deal of hurrying and skurrying on the enemy's part, and some of his cavalrymen pushed their way in the dim light along the road across our front to find our right flank; but they never got away again to report what they discovered; and when a little later their bugles sounded the recall, their horses, some of them limping, went away alone.

Old Dave, an instructed, experienced, and thorough soldier, understood very well that he had to do with the advance of Lee's army; but he counted upon the gloom of night as likely to afford him a chance to get away, and believed that, as the place we were in was difficult for cavalry, he could hold it till the time of gloom came. And all passed as he thought; for though three or four squadrons of cavalrymen came into the village, the commanding officer surveyed our position very deliberately, and discreetly left us alone, satisfied, perhaps, that we were safe there till daylight and sure to be his game then.

And indeed the chances were that the next day would be a troublesome one for us; since, as we were really making a flank-march to the enemy's advance, it was probable there were as many at other points on the road ahead of us as there were here, for there were roads parallel to the one by which the enemy had reached this place, and we were ten miles from the gap.

Prospects were gloomy, therefore. Should we be caught here in the morning, we must be cut up and forced to surrender; should we push on, we must apparently fall into the enemy's hands at another point. And yet the danger was not apparent enough to authorize the blinking of our orders and moving northward. Our only hope was that a rest here of an hour would refresh us for a rapid night-march in which we might slip through the enemy's fingers reached out to grasp us. We must therefore lull

his vigilance somewhat and act as if we intended to
stay here.

So the pieces were stacked, and the boys were
ordered to kindle fires and get their coffee and make
themselves as comfortable as possible.

At this time the night-air was filled with the wild
music of the hungry mule. If the reader is not
familiarly acquainted with this animal and has not
heard him call at night for his over-due rations, he
is ignorant of the most wonderful noise that is common in camps—a noise that in the tonic scale of a
soldier's life occupies about three fourths of the
whole, the other fourth being made up of artillery,
musketry, and brass bands.

But it is when the rain and the cold and a marshy
landscape are added to his other discomforts of hunger, weariness, and impatience that the mule does
himself full justice with his voice and "shoots his
mouth" with glory. He needs to be in such a
country as the Chickahominy runs through, and to
be about two days ahead of the commissary, to be
raised to that height of mulish passion in which he
pours forth his whole soul mainly through his nose
in a protest that startles the wilderness with insane
echoes, which cannot tell whether they are answer-
ing the sneezing of a locomotive or the hooting and
diabolical laughter of thousands of tormented fiends.

Now, we were supplied on this march with an unusual number of wagons, which we had had the
good fortune to pick up on the way,—for all Virginia
was full of abandoned property of that sort, mostly

our own,—and had about twenty mules; and when these mules began to pour forth their hungry hallelujah, a good idea occurred to Dave. He sent word immediately that the mules should not be fed. He then had them driven in groups of five behind the line up and down its length and as far to the left and right as the country was clear, so that their noise was multiplied, or distributed rather: and the commander in front of us was an unreasonable fellow if he did not report that there were mules enough there to haul rations and ammunition for at least two brigades.

Finally the mules were fed, for it was necessary that their melody should be suppressed by a sense of satisfaction before we began to move again; but the ruse was probably effective, for we were left very much to ourselves. At nine we were on the road again. It was then pitch dark, and would apparently continue so, for it was not very clear; and we pushed forward as lively as crickets, and the head of the column reached White Plains near midnight. Pembroke with the rear left Salem at about ten, apparently undiscovered and leaving fires that would burn for two or three hours.

At White Plains the intelligent contraband put in an appearance, and the cavalry straggler was abundantly present; and from their united sources of information it was but too certain that the enemy was at Georgetown and in full possession of the road to the gap. The cavalry said that our forces were nowhere near the gap on the other side of the mountains. All that news was tough for us.

From White Plains there is a road northward to a little place called Hopeville on the western slope of the hills, and at that place there is a road over the mountain ; and Dave promptly decided to go that way. Our march on this road was through a pretty bit of country that under the light of the stars lost no charms it had, and acquired some that it did not really possess ; for it is the peculiar quality of the witchery of night that it works in concert with the imagination, and helps to give to any scene the tone of our own thoughts, which the literal light of day with its naked truth always contradicts and denies, like a bumptious quidnunc.

Soldiers are practical enough when the time comes, yet they are also the most sentimental fellows in the world ; and in a scene like that they will cover five miles easier than they will one on a flat road in a swampy country. Dave reached the crest of the ridge about daylight, and rested there, and the next day marched down and succeeded in joining a portion of the force that was fooling around Stonewall Jackson.

But Pembroke and his company in the rear had met with a mischance, due to the act of a teamster : and it will be conceded by every person of experience that a teamster is the most certain type of the foul fiend in boots. Next to a mule, a mule-driver is the least reasonable and tractable, the most addicted to total depravity, of animated creatures.

Nay, it is not certain but the mule-driver surpasses the mule himself in that, having caught by association the perverse vein of that animal's inclinations and impulses, he applies that spirit of perversity with the superior ingenuity of human nature. As the impulses of teamsters were known, it did not surprise Pembroke, nor the fellows generally in Company H, when it was discovered at dawn that the rest of the battalion was not ahead of them, and that they had been switched off the road in the night.

On this march the wagons had come in the rear of the battalion—or all of the battalion except Company H, and that company was behind the wagons, with orders to follow them; and the duty of the front files of that company was simply to keep their noses against the hind wheels of the last wagon, while the last files trailed far behind in order to give the earliest intimation if the enemy should appear in pursuit. Dave had been up and down the line from front to rear a dozen times in the first two or three hours; but finding all right, and having confidence in Pembroke, he had eventually remained quietly with the advance.

Now, a few miles north of White Plains a road turns to the left out of the Hopewell road, and to the eyes of a teamster, perverse as above described, that road had a seductive aspect; and of his own motion he simply, and without a word said to anybody, turned into it from the straight road, and thus put astray everybody that was behind him; nor had

those behind any means whatever of knowing that
the continuity of the line was broken. At daylight this fellow excused himself by a story that he
was half asleep on his mule and thought this was
the right road.

Company H was thus in the wilderness of Virginia alone; but fortunately one of the wagons with
it had some commissary's stores, and the other some
ammunition, and there were spades and axes in one
of them also. Some fellows were sent out to skyugle around the district and fetch in all the darkies
they could find; and the darkies, examined as to the
roads, cleared up the problem as to where the company was. It was on the road from White Plains
to Aldie—a road that reached the crest of the
mountains therefore, at a point ten or twelve miles
north of where the battalion passed it; and Pembroke could not hear of any roads that crossed, save
one many miles north of where he was.

But everybody had now been on foot about
twenty hours, and rest was indispensable. They
must sleep where they were. If they moved by
noon and got on that cross-road by night it would
get them to Hopewell next day, and the enemy
would probably then be there; if they counter-
marched expeditiously by the road they came they
might march right into the enemy's camp.

There seemed no chance of safety but to push on
for Aldie; and to take a good rest where they were
was a prime necessity for a rapid march to that
place.

CHAPTER IV.

BEFORE sunrise, that day, every fire by which the
boys in Company H had gone to sleep was not only
dead out, but even the little heaps of cinders and
ashes were beaten down level by the pelting rain,
which came suddenly and fell pitilessly; for far to
the east of the mountain there had been firing all
day long the day before, and the rarefaction of the
atmosphere so produced had stirred a movement in
this direction of all the vagabond vapors, and some
from the east, sailing low, had caught on the ridge
above the heads of our friends, and come down on
the western slope like a little deluge.

How it does rain when there is war!

One never knows how much it rains until he has
put on a uniform and given up the customary
shelter of houses, omnibuses, cabs and umbrellas,
and the habit of sleeping in bed, and taken to the
woods, the roads and the ditches, and the occasional
lee side of a haystack, or an outhouse, with a sheet
of India-rubber as his only shelter. Then, indeed,
he discovers that it rains always more or less, and
that the world is full of the noise of the pattering
drops as they beat on every surface presented, from

the great canopies of green leaves to the glistening
India-rubber cloak of the tall sentry down the road.

Blessed be the memory of the fellow who first
subdued to human uses that noble gum which we
call India rubber! How they got on with their
wars in the ages before this substance was spread
into blankets, ponchoes, cloaks, and overcoats is a
mystery. Perhaps they had their primitive contrivances,—sheepskins with the wool on, and kindred rain-defying raiment,—but all these must have
been to the India-rubber coat much as the bow and
arrow to a rifle; and wars must often have petered
out altogether by the mere intervention of rheumatism.

Here again is a point in which the world does
but little justice to its heroes. We have heard of
the charges of the Old Guard, and of its adamantine
squares; but how little have we heard of the rheu-
matisms it endured !

Our fellows on the slope of the mountain just lay
like fellows in the same circumstances from time
immemorial, and let the rain pelt itself out. On
ordinary occasions of bivouac, in the absence of
rain, the soldier spreads his gum blanket on the
earth, and lies upon that wrapped in his woollen
blanket; for then the gum is a defence from the
dampness of the earth. He keeps it between him
and the enemy, and the enemy is on the under side.
But when the rain comes,—presto ! the enemy has
then developed himself in heavy force on the other
side, and the small assault of dampness from be-

neath is no longer worthy thought. So everybody changes position with his blanket, doubles himself in a little knot on the earth, spreads his blanket of India rubber over him, and sleeps on, unconscious of the little streams that find their way under the edge.

And that was the way they slept here. All along the edge of the road and in the wood were knobby, irregular black spots with square edges, made of the spread-out India-rubber blankets, which looked as if some one had distributed on the fair face of nature rather plentifully the "beauty-spots" of an ancient coquette. Under each of these lay at least one soldier, and under some two or three.

Pembroke and Willoughby were better off than the others; for at the first tap of the rain they had got up from the ground and crept into one of the wagons, and thus, though the roof over their heads was leaky, it was a great improvement on the open sky when the whole visible heaven is like no other rose so much as the rose of a watering-pot.

Reveille was sounded at about nine, and that cheery medley of quaint old musical themes enlivened the wet camp a little. But the boys came up slowly; for though one might suppose that such uncomfortable beds would be abandoned with alacrity, it commonly proves otherwise. In truth, fellows have to get themselves up from the wet earth by instalments, and with care as to the kinks in their backs; for if they didn't take these kinks in their right and appropriate succession, they might get themselves in a snarl. It is a point related to mechanical science to get up successfully when every half-inch of your length is the seat of a separate rheumatism.

Fires, also, were slow. It was near noon before the company was on foot, and it had only marched about four miles ere it came to a wide mountain-torrent which crossed the road at right angles between steep, craggy sides, and over which there was no bridge. That important structure had been destroyed on some critical occasion in some former retreat. Now, the boys could have been put over this obstruction on a single timber, which any one of the tall trees about them would have supplied. But the mules and wagons needed a bridge; consequently Pembroke was again tempted to abandon these wagons, as he had been upon the first discovery of his unpleasant position, and at the thought that, but for them, he could perhaps rejoin the column in a few hours by a march across the country.

But the abandonment of material is defeat, and the point of pride involved controlled him. He decided he would build a bridge. Consequently the few axes were out, and the whole company was soon busy at this wet labor. Half a dozen chestnuts, that made forty-foot sticks, were chopped and trimmed in an extremely little while; for the tradition of George Washington has descended to the nation, and every boy is born with a little hatchet in his hand, which he early changes for the more effective axe; and our fellows were experts with woodman's tools.

And as the men with the axes went on and dropped the trees pointed out to them, the others carried to their places those already down. Only one serious difficulty presented itself, which was the placing the first timber across the chasm. We overcame that in this way: All the mule-traces fastened together made a sling, which was rove over the branch of an old chestnut that, growing at the banks of the stream, had grown well out across it, so that one long, heavy limb, about twenty feet above our heads, seemed like a giant arm reached out to help us. With the sling passed over that and one end fastened about the middle of our first timber, the boys hove away on the other end of the sling, and as the weight of the timber was thus suspended, a baby could almost have put it in its place. We cheered that little achievement with much spirit, because to some of the fellows this had seemed an insuperable obstacle, as we seemed to be without machinery; though others knew that the Major's ingenuity was always equal to such difficulties.

Other timbers were run out on that one and put in their places. Four were thus put at intervals across-stream, and then lighter ones across these, till a roadway was made; and on this roadway was spread a thick carpet of pine twigs, held in place by wet clay thrown liberally from either side.

Much of the afternoon had been consumed in this labor; and when the command was over and the bridge destroyed again, only a short march was made beyond ere the night came; and though the rain then no longer fell, the roadway was flooded, and the chance to make distance on such a route without daylight was very hopeless. Therefore the company was halted for the night, in the expectation that a good rest and an early start would prove more advantageous in the end.

Next day a good march was made, and the prospect was that the command would get east of the mountain that night.

Meantime events had gone forward rapidly in that eastern valley. Stonewall Jackson had not been crushed as he might have been by the whole weight of the Army of the Potomac. Between incapacity and indecision that opportunity had slipped away. Other corps of Lee's army had succeeded in joining him; and, admirably handled by their commanders, the hardy tatterdemalions of the Confederacy had made another tough day for our boys at what was called the second Bull Run battle. Once more the people in Washington were gratified with a battle in which the possession of the city seemed at stake, and which was gained by the Southern troops; for this result pleased the people of the place, who were all in sympathy with the South, and it gladdened some men in the government who secretly hoped the rebels might get Washington and destroy it, so that a Northern city might become the seat of the national government.

As a result of that battle the whole Union army

moved in precipitate retreat upon its base; and the whole Southern army, sweeping forward to the invasion of Maryland, filled the valley, and part of its cavalry was actually at Aldie on the afternoon when Pembroke was hastening toward that place up the western side of the mountain.

Fortunately this was discovered before our boys got within reach of that cavalry.

"Contrabands" came in with the information. They generally did in cases of that nature. Southern people who suppose that the negro was faithful to slavery, and Northern people who suppose he did nothing to help us out in the war, never reflect what it was to have always near a people who surrounded the enemy like flies, and could come away as unnoticed, and come into our lines and tell the fact it was supremely necessary for us to know.

As soon as it was positively known that this report was true, Pembroke determined to try and reach Winchester, in the expectation that a resolute effort would be made to hold that place, and that he could get there before it should be abandoned. But this cavalry at Aldie might be in the way there also, and he understood that he must avoid highroads and would not be secure for a moment till he got to the Blue Ridge.

He had at least fifteen miles before him, and hoped to make it by noon.

Fortunately the region is a good marching country and a mesh of by-roads; so that if there seemed any likelihood of danger from the cavalry, the command could be easily put out on a by-road and lose little if any time with regard to its route; while if driven altogether to one side from the road to Ashby's Gap, which was the shortest, it could get through at Snicker's.

We made that run for Winchester with a rush. There was some pleasure in it also; for on those picturesque roads between pleasant corn-fields and reaches of woods that were not altogether a wilderness, we were in a country then little touched by the war: and this was a treat to us. There were not only larger green apples than we found elsewhere, but there were other unusual dainties.

Whenever a country has been torn up by war, every pleasant addition to daily diet that might be bought at a farm-house is gone, and the very landscape itself is a ghastly scene of standing chimneys from which the houses they belonged to have been burned away. Even the fences have been turned into fire wood.

Merrily enough, therefore, we went on, for troops that move through a picturesque country in pleasant weather, without unreasonable disquiet, and with just enough consciousness of the enemy to keep up an easy alert, have the picnic side of campaigning life. Nobody grumbled, therefore, that that day's march was kept on beyond the time of ordinary marches, and that the deepening shadows of the twilight found us still on foot.

All that day Willoughby had been different from what he had been in the few days our fellows had

seen him. He was extravagantly gay or lapsed into
continued silence. He was anxious, eager, uneasy,
nervous. This difference had caused some quiet
comment in the ranks; and once when they were
hidden in the woods, old Maltby had almost unconsciously kept the muzzle of his rifle within
about a foot of Willoughby's head for half an hour.
Willoughby might by a shout have brought a
crowd in on us, but he would never, have shouted
again.

It was at Willoughby's suggestion that the last
turn had been made which had brought us upon the
pleasantest road yet seen. It was a turn aside from
the straight route over the mountains, and it ran
through a district which perhaps owed its immunity
from war's ravages to the fact that it was quite
apart from any highroad that led to any important
point. Several times since we had entered this
region, which was about four in the afternoon, Pembroke had been on the point of ordering a halt for
the night; but each time Willoughby had persuaded
him to keep on a little yet, on the promise of some
pleasant hospitality just a few miles ahead.

"Some friends of mine live on this road; and if
we can pass the night near them, there's not only
good 'chicken-fixin's' in the kitchen for us, but also
a good bottle of wine in the cellar."

Such was the promise Willoughby had made several times that afternoon; and it presented a great
temptation to the mind of Pembroke, as the reader
will readily understand if any considerable part of

his life has been filled with the monotonous diet of salt-horse and hard-tack, moistened only with the warm water that dribbles down. the Virginia ditches, or with the same water turned into an acrid decoction of camp coffee.

Pembroke was just beginning to doubt whether duty toward the men and his own inclination were not in opposition—whether, in fact, he was justified in pushing this march farther in order to procure a trivial treat of good rations for himself—when, behold! the goal was before them.

They were full in front of Braxton House, and a pleasant surprise it was.

Beyond a lawn so wide and spacious that it was rather an upland meadow than a lawn arose the rarest of all sights in the State of Virginia, a really fine house; a structure whose various additions and attachments rambled away into the comfortable circumstances of a farm, but which presented in the foreground the stately proportions and design of a mansion where wealth and taste might find themselves in a congenial home.

Virginia houses are as a rule monotonous structures. There has come down to us from the colonial days a tone of romantic reference to the splendor of life in the Old Dominion, which we in the war found to be the most baseless of fictions; for the common centre of life in the sunny South is a ground-floor of two or three square rooms, with a kitchen in a "lean-to;" three or four cramped bedchambers in the one upper story; and a piazza across the front of the house—good homes for the people, but not things to glorify in an architectural sense. Men and women were happy in those houses. Grand boys were bred there; and on the pleasant piazzas in the moonlight nights lovely girls listened with happy delight to the old, old story. But with all that, they were a disappointment to fellows who had gathered somehow in the atmosphere of our history a notion of Virginia as the place of a more glorious kind of existence.

Braxton House was, however, one of the fine exceptions; and its harmonious proportions and the good effect of its form and position filled the beholder with pleasure; and in that house and in the grounds about it one might easily enough imagine could have been passed such days of baronial splendor as the Southern romancers dwell upon.

CHAPTER V.

As soon as Company H came into view beyond
the little curtain of woods between the house and
the road below it, a sort of far-away animation became visible about the house. Chickens started in
an instinctive stampede for refuge, putting their
length to the earth in a long desperate lope; some
pigs that had been loose in the wood beside the
house snorted and hustled away through the low
bushes, having heard no doubt that we were fond of
fresh meat; half a dozen dogs bayed heavily from
unseen kennels; and old aunties and uncles hobbled
out from their hiding-places, and queer little pickaninnies peeped around the corners of shanties and
pigpens and garden-gates.

Word spread through the house that the "Linkum
sojers" were near, and more than one soul was filled
with dismay at this confirmation of the news already
abroad in that region to the effect that this district
was once more the seat of war. Dr. Braxton, his
sister, and his daughter Phœbe went to front windows to survey the scene. Phœbe, quicker than the
others, caught sight of Willoughby on the lawn, and
in another moment the bolts of the front door were

drawn with nervous haste, and Phœbe rushed into the arms of Willoughby, already on the piazza.

Now, this was the fair lady to marry whom Willoughby had been on his way when taken; and his tempting offer of pleasant hospitality for the Major was therefore not entirely unrelated to his own desires and anxieties; for, to do him simple justice, it must be said that he was not more moved by the wish to see his sweetheart than by his eagerness to calm the inquietude that had been caused by his failure to appear at the time he was looked for.

How warm was his welcome may be imagined, as well as the sentiments then indulged toward us.

While Willoughby with his friends inside explained the mystery of his failure to come at the time he was expected, Pembroke formed the camp at the lower slope of the wide lawn, near the little street, and posted pickets up and down the road and behind the house toward the mountain; for he did not imagine that our march would remain indefinitely unknown to the enemy, and he considered trouble possible.

Fires were cracked up in a marvellously short time; for the first thought in such a halt is, not rest, but cookery.

Between eight and nine, Pembroke and Wood, the lieutenant, the only other commissioned officer with us, were invited into the house to "take a meal."

Having made a hasty toilet down by the stream, they were ready when the word came, and moved

4

with alacrity. They were shown into the dining-room, which opened upon one end of the piazza and had been planned with a view to a larger family than usually sat in it. There was, due perhaps to its deep-colored mahogany and its heavy simplicity, an old-fashioned style about it, very agreeable and quiet, and not fitted to distract attention from what was on the table.

Everybody was there: old Dr. Braxton himself, an acute man whose keen face was softened by the effect of his gray hair, and who was a better man than he pretended to be; Aunt Hetty Chichester, an irrepressible old rebel; and the beautiful Miss Phœbe, with happy Willoughby near her. The neat colored girls were trim in their best calicoes, and Aunt Hetty's best "chany" teacups were drawn up in column of companies.

"We should be well pleased, gentlemen," said Braxton, coming forward with a ceremonious air, "if we could give you a welcome and a treat that would make you forget the fatigues of such a day."

They both said they were sure of his good-will, and equally confident of his ability to give it effect; and then there were ceremonious presentations all around, and they sat down.

In view of all the circumstances, the Major and Wood could not but consider their welcome warm. They could not fail to perceive that the others were those whom the fates intended should be happy, and that they themselves were the villains of the drama; The representatives of evil destiny that stood in the way of the fulfilment of all pleasant hopes. And the Major said:

"Certainly it is generous for you to be able to see us with any equanimity whatever."

"Why," said Aunt Hetty, peceiving quicker than the others that Pembroke was thinking of his unpleasant relation as the inconvenient enemy, "we know that war is war, and that no gentleman would spoil sport if he could help it."

"We are very glad indeed that you appreciate the case so accurately," said Pembroke. While the fair Phœbe, with just a trace of timidity, turned a glance of deprecation toward Aunt Hetty, possibly in fear that that bold orator might go farther than was desirable in the statement of the delicate position.

"We understand," said Dr. Braxton, "that when gentlemen are sworn to a cause they cannot put their casual inclinations in the balance against it."

"We know that you would not have stopped our boy if you could have acted on your own impulses," said Aunt Hetty.

"Shall I give you coffee, sir?" interrupted Phœbe from her vantage-ground behind the grand array of white and rose-colored porcelain, and in a voice indescribably musical and sympathetic.

Pembroke thought he would take some coffee later, and would for the moment cultivate a more intimate acquaintance with the wine, which was announced as Madeira, and which they naturally thought should be old Madeira.

Dr. Braxton said it was old Madeira, "part of the cargo of a ship lost on Hatteras about the time of the revolution."

Aunt Hetty hoped that Madeira was not so fatal to men as it appeared to be to ships. She had never heard of any that did not come from a wreck.

So the Madeira went round—a liquid topaz in its cut-glass receptacle; for the doctor was an old-fashioned man and decanted his wine. He regarded the time-stained label and the dust-coated bottle as the contrivances of a vulgar period which demanded other guarantees of the age of wine besides a gentleman's word and the wine itself.

And thus they steered safely away from themes that were always difficult and dangerous in companies so made up. It was the standard evening meal of the times; a culinary glory that everybody loved to come upon. There was but one dish—a fricaseed chicken with cream sauce; but that and the company together made a festival.

Pembroke was especially interested in the quiet observation of Willoughby's fiancée. Toward Pembroke her air was one of gracious and amiable indifference, in which there was no sacrifice of politeness, but from which one feels what an immeasurable distance, in the lady's eyes, there is between himself and a happier man. In this the Major saw only the fair damsel's devotion to her one ideal, and the disposition of a true woman not to care particularly to shine in the eyes of all the men she might meet.

Wood was that human wonder, a silent Irish-man. Silent ordinarily, that is; but when the bottle had passed and repassed between him and Braxton, till they seemed like two fellows in the line of bat-tle using the same ramrod, he became fluent, and the bravery of Southern men was the topic.

"The Confederate soldier," he said, "makes a great deal of nyse when he fights; but he fights well, and against any troops but ours he would be a conqueror." This he said with his deliberate drawl, with a pause between each word, and a slow utterance, as if, being a man of few words, he would make them go as far as possible.

Braxton's vocabulary was also thawed out, and they became a gay and cheery party and forgot in the pleasures of the hour both yesterday and to-mor-row; but this was after the Madeira-bottle had been relieved two or three times. They lingered long at the table,—as who would not if his ordinary fare was "salt horse" by the wayside?—and then they ad-journed to the piazza.

By and by there was an almost imperceptible distribution. Wood went down to the camp; the doctor disappeared entirely; Phœbe and Wil-loughby sat together in that obscure part of the piazza embowered by the heavy-growing vines; and Aunt Hetty seized upon Pembroke with the will of one who has not met a conversational creature for many a day, and rattled at him her whole bud-get of stored-up fancies.

"It is my opinion," said the old lady, "that men

are women with the emotions left out. What do you say to that?"

"Perhaps the thought is just; but I should have stated it from another point of view."

"As life is a show, and we sit at the windows and look out upon it, one person only can occupy one place; therefore everybody's point of view is different. But come, what is yours?"

"Well, I should say that women are men with the emotions added."

"That is different, and yet the same. It disputes which is the standard type, but admits my account of the essential variation. But now, on your honor as a gentleman and a soldier, is not that addition the one point that gives all the value?"

"Aunt Hetty," said Pembroke,—for in the frolicsome humor of the moment they had caught up this familiar family style,—"you are making this case very difficult. Only a few moments since you reasoned with me on a metaphysical basis; now you appeal to my honor as a gentleman and a soldier for my opinion about the ladies."

"No, sir; about woman: and this is an evasion. But how do these characters differ as to truth?"

"Well, a metaphysician cannot regard the poetical side of the case, and a gentleman and a soldier must regard that side mainly."

Resolute not to have any nonsense in this conversation, yet a little cajoled by the Major's tone, she said :

"Well, then, resolve the doubt in any of these characters."

"In all of them," said the Major. "From the stand-point of a gentleman and a soldier, your view of the value of the emotions is accurate. They are the most precious part of the most precious creature. But a philosopher would probably say they are an addition a little like that of one more in a boat already perilously full."

"Well, they do swamp it sometimes. But I'll tell you this: there never was a first-rate gentleman in the world who was not possessed in a great degree of this feminine attribute. What I understand people to mean when they say a man has heart is that he is in a great degree under the influence of his emotions."

"Well, it perhaps means that, if anything," said the Major.

"It means that," said the old lady. "The moralities and intellectualities and what not, are so many endeavors to root out our merely human impulses, as if those were weeds in the garden and we wanted all the room for those rare plants. If we succeed in this weeding, we make of a gay, good-hearted youngster one of those correct, intolerable creatures like the good boys in Sunday-school romances. Nobody is endurable to me who has not in him a spice of what the world thus treats as vice, for the burst of evil now and then shows that the old human fountain has not gone dry. How I do adore Faust; and Goethe, who had the courage to make human

weakness the basis of heroism! For to me it seems
the final test of a man's courage that he dare go
anywhere to satisfy the impulses that are in him."

"Well, that's going a great way," said the
Major.

"Not very; indeed, if it were a longer journey
more would travel that way. People arrive at
Faust's goal too soon. The compensations of the
wayside are therefore not an equivalent for the end.
Every hour of the weary days we sit here," said the
old lady, suddenly changing her tone, "and wonder what is to happen. I cannot but make this
comparison: that the South is a kind of national
woman, and the North a national man. And it
fills me with fear for the future."

Pembroke was afraid to answer. This was delicate ground; and he only sat still while the old
lady ran on.

"Yes," she said, "the North is a masculine
giant, with overwhelming cold intellect and the
force it gives, and with the emotions—the heart—
bred out. It fills the idea of that myth—of the
giant that had no heart in his body. But the South
—passionate, impulsive, emotional through and
through—cannot, because of this very quality, use to
the best point even the force it has."

"But," hesitated the Major, "if the absence of
the emotions implies a defective nature—"

"Yes, yes," she said, interrupting, "I know
where you will come out; my own reasoning leads
to the point that the South should be the superior

in virtue of what she is.   But I did not mean superiority as determined by the test of mere force.
Besides, I do not try my country by this reasoning
to find it in fault; but by the position in which
such reasoning finds my country I try the world,
and the age in which we live.   Nations perhaps
thrive as they are fitted to the age; and if the South
fails, it will be because the age is a bad, hollow, vile
utilitarian one."

Good old Mrs. Chichester had set out in a mere
spirit of gossip, but she had inadvertently gone too
far, and become too deeply involved in the current
of her own thoughts; and, afraid of her nerves,
she got up and stepped quietly and swiftly away
through one of the open windows.

Aunt Hetty was gone.   Dr. Braxton had not been
seen for an hour or more, and Pembroke could hear
near him only the soft murmuring of the voices of
Willoughby and Phœbe in the deep gloom of the
vines at the other end of the piazza.

He concluded that the day was over, and thought
of sleep.   Making a little tour across the lawn
to where the men lay, he saw that all was tranquil
there; that the sentries were at their posts up and
down the road; and that scarcely a sound was to be
heard save from the little camp-fires where the
company darkies had cooked the supper: and there,
their numbers recruited by darkies of the Braxton
family, the happy contrabands made themselves
merry with music.

Then he returned to his end of the piazza, and

stretched himself for slumber where the thoughtful
Hayward had put a saddle for a pillow and a blanket for a bed.

It was the opinion of the ingenious Polyænus
that Bacchus conquered India very easily because
he went there not as a conqueror but as a jovial
merry-maker, hiding all things that could indicate
an offensive intention under cover of some part of
the apparatus of delight. Ribbons and finery hid
his weapons, and the golden cone of the thyrsis
wherever it appeared was but a sheath to a spear-
point. He put the spirit of conquest in a thin picnic envelope of hilarity and joy.

Perhaps that stratagem was borrowed from nature. Because so much that is deadly is beautiful
we might imagine that at least as much that is
beautiful is related to the deadly. Is there a more
beautiful line in the world than that traced in the
green and gold of the spotted snake? And if conquest puts on the forms of hilarity and delight,
must we not fancy that hilarity and delight come
to us always as the stratagems of some sort of conquest?

Some such absurd notions as these jostled one
another in the brain of Captain Pembroke, in that
uncertain intellectual world between thought and
dream, as he lay in the little rose-covered piazza,
weary with the labors and excitement of the day, in
a reverie that sloped steeply toward deep sleep.

It was a quiet, beautiful night, starry but without a moon, and a fresh dewy air came in between

the vines loaded with fragrance. Some little sound
of voices still came from the lovers near by; for
Willoughby and Phœbe were not disposed to cut
short the delights of an unhoped-for interview for
the mere sake of physical repose. Out toward the
camp a few fires smouldered; but all was still.

One might have imagined that this was thousands
of miles away from any land torn up by war. Even
the sentry who paced to and fro near by, his foot-
fall broken by the velvet sward, seemed a very
tranquil, peaceful presence.

Why, then, was Pembroke, just on the edge of
his slumber,—at the outpost as it were of a good
night's rest,—troubled with fancies that behind the
pleasant hospitality he had enjoyed in the Braxton
house there might be danger? Could there be
treachery in such people? No; and yet these fancies slipped into and tangled his otherwise pleasant
dreams.

CHAPTER VI.

COMPANY H FIGHTS ITS WAY OUT.

MAJOR PEMBROKE was suddenly awakened from a deep sleep by the heavy hand of Sergeant Hayward on his arm. He started up, and the sergeant said:

"Will you come a little away from the house, sir?"

He seized his hat, sword, and revolver, and followed the sergeant a dozen paces.

"There's cavalry coming up the road we marched on to day," said Hayward; "and an old darky down by the camp-fire says they're Ashby's men, and that word was sent to them to-night from the house here to come over."

This report did not surprise Pembroke. He had thought or dreamed so much that might naturally lead up to it that it came rather as a confirmation of what was already known than as fresh intelligence.

"What sort of a fellow is the darky?"

"An old sober fellow who belongs in the neighborhood here."

"Who reports the cavalry?"

"Hagadorn, the corporal."

"Turn the company out. Have the men drawn up as rapidly as possible, and send Lieutenant Wood here."

"Yes, sir;" and the sergeant was gone.

Pembroke had by this time collected himself, and buckled on his sword; and as he waited for Wood in the gloom about twenty paces from the house, he thought with a lively impatience rather than with rage upon the apparent treason of those whose hospitality he had sought for their pleasure, not his own, and whose act might this night cost the lives of half his men and the liberty of all.

"It is very dangerous to trust an enemy in war, sir," said Wood at his elbow.

"Mr. Wood," he said, "if these people have really brought the cavalry down upon us, as seems probable, that may not be the whole of their plan."

"Likely there's more behind, sir," said Wood.

"And we must be beforehand with them, and have no unnecessary tenderness for them."

"Indade, sir, if we wanted a light to fight by, the blaze of this house would illuminate a fine bit of country."

"Not that," said Pembroke, "but this: If there is a great deal of cavalry, we cannot fight it on this clear level; but we may be able to get away from it in the gloom; or higher up the mountain, in the woodier or rougher regions, we may find positions in which we can stand off any number of them."

"It is very true, sir."

"But if these people remain in the house when we leave, to communicate all they know of our force, condition, and isolation, and just which way we have gone, it will be much the worse for us."

"Must keep the enemy in ignorance, sir."

"Therefore take half a dozen files of men and get every soul out of the house, white, black, or yellow, —go gently with the ladies,—and hurry them all up the mountain—no time to lose. The road we came on winds at the north side, returns behind the house here, and climbs the mountain with many doubles. You can get into it from the rear by a little lane."

"I know the way, sir," said Wood, who had indeed inspected all the strategic relations of the house before they sat down to supper.

"I will come behind you with the rest in case there appears to be more cavalry than we can fight on this plateau. Take care to keep in communication; for if it seems best to fight here, I may need your men."

"I will take care, sir," said the deliberate lieutenant.

Pembroke hastened away through an orchard to the point at which the cavalry must first reach his lines; but before he was half way there the sharp report of a rifle broke the midnight silence, and then came another and another. The pickets were firing upon the advancing enemy.

There was a considerable body of cavalry, and owing to the wonderful stillness of the night in this isolated bit of country the men on guard had heard the jingle of the cavalry-sabres against the saddles at a great distance, and thus were very early aware of the approach of this force. This discovery was facilitated by the lay of the country, which was such that often a point three or four miles away by the road was only half a mile away across some gulch. Consequently the advance was not a surprise, or rather it was a surprise to the cavalry; and when two troopers in front of the force had been called upon to halt and had not given a satisfactory response, the pickets had fired, and these first troopers had gone to the right-about in a hurry.

Pembroke leaped into the road behind his men just as a hastily-formed skirmish-line of the troopers was descried coming forward as if to explore this obstacle. He withdrew his men from the road to the little elevation beside it in the orchard through which he had come, and held them quietly there. But the cavalrymen, not making out this manoeuvre in the heavy gloom, came on coolly, and at twenty paces opened fire at that point in the road from which our men had delivered their first fire. They were permitted to advance until they were fairly opposite to our fellows in the orchard, and then our boys gave them a fire which knocked that small skirmish-line into a cocked hat.

Immediately our men were double-quicked across the orchard to the camp, the pickets down the road were called in, and the whole command was put in motion to follow Lieutenant Wood; for Pembroke had learned enough in his short visit to the pickets to convince him that the open plateau about Braxton House was no place for Company H on this occasion.

As the men stepped promptly away toward the

lane that led to the mountain-road, the Major heard
a bugle-note, and the gallant cheer of a regiment, at
that point where the pickets had halted the enemy,
and then the thunder of horses' hoofs and clamor of
rattling accoutrements, as the whole force of cavalry
charged down to clear the road. One of those turns
in the road already referred to was of use here; for
while the spot where the pickets had been posted was
but a few hundred yards away across the orchard,
the cavalry would have to trot a mile and a half to
get to the gate of Braxton House; and if they found
the trail up the mountain immediately, they could
not follow it rapidly.

Nearly the whole vocabulary of Southern elo-
quence was exhausted upon Lieutenant Wood before
he got the family fairly on the road. But the temper of that officer was not in the least ruffled by the
torrent of words.

Phœbe had not uttered a syllable, for she had a
natural apprehension that there might be some new
danger for Willoughby in all this. She had heard
stories of prisoners killed to prevent rescue or
escape. She thought it might be such a case, and
she went like one in a trance, mounted on an old
family nag, while Willoughby walked beside her,
holding her little white hand desperately in his
own.

Old Braxton was so recklessly savage in speech
that Wood put him in particular charge of a man
he could depend upon, with an intimation that he
would hold him personally responsible for the safe

delivery at the next camp of this "unnecessarily energetic old gentleman."

Aunt Hetty Chichester and a dozen old aunties and uncles and pickaninnies were the troublesome part of the *cortege*, but by patience and resolution all were put on the way, and moved rapidly up the mountain.

Pembroke went through the house, found not a soul there, and followed his men through the lane, himself the last file-closer. He was himself "the whipsnapper to the rear-guard," as old Keyes used to say.

Our fellows had a start of about half an hour; for the cavalry, having discovered out on the road that it might prove expensive to come forward in too much of a hurry, now came forward deliberately; feeling, perhaps, sure of their prey, but conscious that they might get a fire from us at any step. As soon as they reached the level upon which Company H had been encamped, they swept their line forward rapidly and surrounded the house. It was imagined, apparently, that we were there and intended to hold the place. Time was consumed in making proper dispositions to prevent our escape; then we were summoned to surrender, and it was discovered that we were gone.

"No, no," said Wood, with an apostrophe in the direction of the enemy, "we are not there. We have tried the game of fighting in tinder-boxes before to-night."

5

They did not hear him, but they made certain of our absence.

Where then were we? Scurrying up and down, to and fro, and hither and thither, was the next resort for the solution of this difficult problem; and at last two of the cavalrymen, finding the mountain-way, followed it rapidly, until they were dropped in the road by the fire of our rear-guard, delivered almost in their faces. Those shots told the story, and soon the whole force was at our heels.

But good use had been made of the time gained. We were now two hundred feet above Braxton House, and the road was rough, stony, and crooked; and a position had been selected in which we could stand off indefinitely ten times as much cavalry as we had just now to deal with. At the end of a steep stretch in the road it turned suddenly, with a sheer mountain-wall at one side and a steep abyss at the other, and above the turn it followed the upper edge of the mountain-wall. Here a section of men posted at the turn could fire fair down the road and sweep it, while others above could loose upon the advancing cavalry an avalanche of loose boulders.

Here it seemed to many of us was the right place to make our fight for good and all; but the Major had learned that yet a little higher up the mountain was a wide plateau which stretched north and south for many miles, and it seemed possible to him that a part of the cavalry, by making a wide detour, could come down on our rear, and that our good corner might prove a trap. He resolved, therefore, only to hold this for delay and push on. Hayward was therefore put in charge of the prisoners, and Wood, who was as resolute a fighter as there was in the army, was put in command here, while the remainder of the company was pushed forward across the plateau.

All this was on foot while they hunted for us below, and when they came up we gave it to them. Between the stones launched down the mountain and the fire of the men posted at the turn, the infernal fiends could not have come up that road; yet the gallant rebels tried it handsomely over and over again; and between their yells and our rifles the mountain-side was a pandemonium of racket for a good hour.

Meanwhile Major Pembroke with the main body of the company pushed on for the point where the definite rise toward the rugged top of the mountain would justify a final stand, but found this difficulty: the region was so far from where the boys were fighting, just below the edge of the plateau, that if they once left this point they could never reach the other before they would be overtaken and ridden down by the cavalry. It would not do to lose them in that way, and a point of resistance or obstruction must be found between these places.

Fortune favored us in this particular.

Much of this plateau was a wide mountain-morass; such a piece of country as is found where the streams from the higher parts of a range discharge themselves on a level and do not find their way out because a rocky edge all around is higher than the middle. Sudden heavy rains flood such regions, and this had recently been overflowed in that way. There was a well-constructed road across the level, but a horse got mired almost anywhere at either side of it.

At a place about two miles from the crest of the plateau there were twenty haystacks, the product, perhaps, of all the level; and distributed all along on one side of the road were many hundred feet of well-piled cordwood.

At this spot we were all halted, and there was some deliberation, while the steady rattle of the fire at the ridge told how coolly the fellows there were giving an account of themselves to the enemy.

Then we stacked arms and carried hay. All the hay was distributed on the road, two or three feet deep, for as far as it would go, which was perhaps five hundred feet—though I hope no mathematical fellow will try this case on me, for it was a dim night, and I will not swear to the distance. Besides, I won't swear to the number or size of the stacks of hay. There might have been twenty-five.

Upon the hay we put wood, every fellow carrying logs on his shoulders. It was chestnut, maple, pine, hickory, and white oak,—the miscellaneous cutting of a mountain country,—and it was thoroughly dry. We scattered it higgledy-piggledy over the hay rough and high, and also for a good way up the road beyond the hay. Hagadorn, the corporal, bossed this job, while the Major galloped away to

cheer up the boys at the crest, and Hayward pushed
the prisoners far away ahead of us across the level.

Between the Major and Lieutenant Wood it was
agreed, at this time, that the Major should give
a signal from the new obstruction when all was
ready there, and that after that signal Wood could
come in with the men at the first good chance he
saw.

Our job was so far advanced when the Major returned that he had to abandon the mule with which
he had ridden to the crest. He could not be got
over the obstruction.

In twenty minutes more we were on the march
again, with orders that half a mile out five files
should be halted till the men from the crest had
passed them, and they were then to come in behind.

Then the signal for Wood was given,—a solitary
rifle-shot,—and the Major sat down to wait for him.
Wood chose a happy moment for his departure,
which was just after the repulse of a very desperate
attempt to storm his stronghold made by the enemy's men on foot. There was always a lapse between their assaults, and he judged that such a lapse
now would give time to get away. He had not
reached the new obstruction, however, before they
found he was gone, as was indicated by the cheer at
the crest, and the rush from there. He got well
behind the obstruction, however, before they came
in sight.

Only Major Pembroke remained at the obstruction. It was late, but there was no moon; or if there

was, she was masked by a heavy coast of clouds which lay low and would dim her radiance for a little longer.

It was an anxious time for the Major as he heard that cheer and rush of the cavalry, and saw Wood's men clambering over the obstruction, several of them badly hurt, and the detachment two short. Then when it was a dead certainty that the whole cavalry would be at this place in ten or fifteen minutes, he went about and rubbed matches and dropped them in the hay.

Slowly the little tongues of fire turned and twisted to one side or another and sought sustenance. In twenty or thirty places they labored in this way for a minute or two, and then it seemed as if they discovered one another and lifted themselves up and spread; and in an incredibly short space of time that whole mass of hay and wood was one fierce blaze.

Behind the cloud of heavy rolling smoke that rose from his well-contrived fire the Major waited with a little calm glee in his soul; for he believed he had beaten them, but could not well feel sure. There might be some fellow there, and probably was, born on this very plateau, and if there was a path across he would know it.

The enemy rode up furiously and fiercely, the joy of success at one point cut short in the rage of disappointment at another.

Some of them rode their horses fairly into the fire, thinking it a thin curtain only which they could gallop through. But they lost their horses and got out themselves badly scorched, for the wood, extremely dry, had soon caught, and the heat was terrible. Other horses, wiser than their masters, could not be spurred in.

"No horse but Beelzebub's own could get through that without breaking his legs, not if he had forty of 'em," said one old trooper; and the truth was recognized. Then they tried desperately the fields at either side, and gave that up; and when at last Pembroke followed his men, the enemy had dismounted and was engaged in the pleasant occupation of making coffee by the fire the Yankees had kindled.

We reached the farther side of the plateau, passed a wide mountain-torrent on a little bridge, sent the bridge into the chasm below with a few axe-strokes, and a mile or two beyond went into camp in a good defensible spot.

It was late and we needed no rocking.

We had left behind us four good men killed by the fire of the cavalry at the crest. Two had died at the crest, and two on this march behind the fire.

They were Corporal Silas Wainwright, and privates Richard Harrison, Ralph Sinclair, and Thomas Dalrymple. Better fellows never wore blue crosses on their caps.

The teamster who had first led us wrong was probably killed by the enemy at Braxton. He was last seen drunk and asleep in one of the outhouses there. At all events, we never saw him after that night.

CHAPTER VII.

ORDERS were given not to make fires in camp that night; which was a very proper precaution, since, as we did not in the least know of the lay of the land except immediately about us, those little centres of human comfort might also prove to be far-seen signals, and would in that case procure for us the attention of any commander of rebel forces that might be out in the valley.

But that night in that high mountain region was sharp; and the nipping and eager air was wet with a cold drizzle that thickened the marrow of our bones.

Ehen! what a glory is a little camp-fire in a night like that! How the cheery crackle of the sticks warms with its very music!

Fire, dear boys, if you know what it is at any time in your houses and homes, on your hearth-stones or in your stoves, you do not perhaps know what it is to a soldier in his bivouac.

If the very planets themselves revolve around a central fire, it is no doubt the original material impulse. But there are other glories in it. What is home but the fire on the hearth-stone, and the happy group about it? At that blaze what souls are light-

ed up with life! But away from home, friends, all
—the fire is often all there is of a fellow's country,
and the blaze of a few bits of wood relights
the lamp of life for the soldier every day in bad
times.

There was, however, one exception to the order
against fires, and one was kindled for the comfort of
the women, since it was not to be supposed they
would have our habit of enduring hardship. This
indulgence was allowed when it was found that
there was a corner in which they could be made
comfortable, and where a fire could be lighted with
a certainty that it could not be seen from even a very
little distance.

There was a dry protected spot, about which the
great tumbled boulders made an almost perfect wall;
and giant pines towered far above this wall of stone
in such a way that their branches would prevent the
view of even a reflection of the fire.

At the farther side of this singular combination
of stones and trees there was a precipitous descent of
several hundred feet, also covered with gnarled and
knotted evergreens growing from crevices of the
rocks. In that place a shelter was made of India-
rubber blankets and pine foliage, and the two ladies
were lodged there. Three men were put on guard
in front of that shelter—not that they were prisoners, but to protect them from intrusion. It was assumed that the inaccessible nature of the other side
was protection enough there.

All this care for the women was taken at night

before we slept, under the Major's orders, and was intended, of course, as a slight compensation to them for the perils and fatigues which had been caused them through no fault of ours. For when the game was once on foot (and their side began it), we could not leave anybody behind who could give information about us; and we had to suppose that these women would, for, even if they were not disposed to do this, information would be extorted from them by threats and terror.

But the old man and Mr. Willoughby had been lodged safely at another part of the camp. They were prisoners.

At about daylight Major Pembroke, apparently upon a mature consideration of all the facts, determined that we should stay where we were for that day at least.

All the information we had of things in the world about us was derived from the darkies who had followed us at night or begun to come in early—and they came that day until they were so numerous that we had to compel them to form a camp of their own at another point on the mountain.

Information of this sort was commonly accurate on main facts, but cloudy on all points of detail, except points as to roads, and paths through the woods, and streams and bridges and villages. But accurate information as to the whereabouts of bodies of the enemy was what we wanted just now, and of that there was very little.

Until we could know just how to move we might

as well stand still, and this would rest us all and give the wounded fellows a chance; so the thoughtful Major let the boys sleep on. As it was now known that there was such a body as ours in that country it would not be well, of course, to stay too many days in one place; and that, as we subsequently knew, the Major did not forget.

No reveille awakened us in camp that day, because the roll of the morning drum re-echoed from the rocky cliffs might have secured for us by day as much attention as the blaze of a fire by night. If we had the enemy all about us, we could get away only by Indian tactics.

And that is how it happened that the two ladies were not aroused by the fife and drum, but first became aware that the camp was on foot by the talk they heard outside their shelter.

How they got through the apprehensions and anxieties of that night it would be difficult to tell; but when we halted and they were put into that safe and comparatively cosey corner, they perhaps slept a little from the mere exhaustion due to so much of a rough run as they had.

But the pleasant assurance that it was day came from the voice of Hayward the sergeant, who was posted at one of the approaches to their corner.

He sang with many variations of an unmusical voice a chant of those days which ever returned to the singular allegation:

> "A soldier's life is always gay—
> Al·ways ga—y!"

And as the incongruity of this declaration with the present circumstances seemed to dawn upon him, he added, in a less rhythmical style:

"Specially 'bout daylight follerin' a wet night and a helter-skelter run in the mountains; when the aforesaid sojer wakes up stiff with the rheumatis, and has to get up slow for fear of breaking into new j'ints if he goes too fast; cold through and through, and wringing wet; with an appetite like an earthquake, and no breakfast, and all the wood too darned wet to burn—

"Too wet to burn — yes, sirree; and what's worse, orders not to burn it: no fires till after rev-er-lee—and, by Jingo, no rev-er-lee!

"I'm 'nation glad I ain't the commander of these troops; for, if I was, some feller'd say I was a fool, and I'd have to lick him.

"Which would be beneath my dignity as an officer. Correct thing would be to hang him up by the thumbs, and that would be hard upon a feller for only telling the truth.

"Upon the whole, it is better as it is, though it's pretty bad."

"What are you growling about, Jake?" said another voice.

Whereupon a third voice said:

"He ain't growlin' about nothin' pertickler; he's amusin' himself with philosophical conversation."

"Growlin'!" said Hayward. "If you call that growlin', you orter hear me when times is hard with the boys. If you call that growlin', what would you call the cheerful voice of the early robin when there ain't no wums? I was only goin' into per-ticklers about the gayety of a soldier's life, and givin' reasons for it."

Hereupon, convinced by all this miscellaneous gabble, that there were plenty on foot about her, the old lady appeared to Hayward and proposed to give him burning sticks from her sheltered fire with which to start his own, upon the sole condition that he should divide the coffee with her and her niece.

"Proposition accepted. Would ha' given you coffee long ago if I'd know'd you wanted it, ma'am," said Hayward.

And that's how the ladies got their first breakfast at "Camp Git-away."

Our boys called that first camp on the mountain-top by that name, because, as they understood it, we had at once got away from the enemy and with the enemy; for in their speech to "git away with" some one was to outwit or outdo him, or in any way to demonstrate your own superiority.

Names for camps which involved humorous fan-cies were always popular with the men, for this was the soldier's fun. It was one of his ways of meet-ing an unpropitious destiny by laughing at it. And even the very littleness of the joke involved some-times helped this effect, because the smallness of the pleasantry with which we meet any given calamity may indicate not so much a paucity of wit as the measure of contempt for the occasion.

We had seven wounded men in camp,—fellows not so badly hurt but that they had been able to keep up,—and at roll-call it was found we were four men short. Some of the darkies who had come in about daylight reported these men dead at different points on the way, and a detail was sent back, guided by the contrabands, to bury our boys.

As for the wounded men, it turned out that old Braxton was a good surgeon, and he volunteered to dress the wounds and care for the wounded if instruments could be obtained from his house. By comparing notes with the darkies it was found that we were not a great way from the house, though the winding road had made the march a long one.

Two adventurous fellows were ready to undertake this errand, and went, accompanied by a darky of the family, with a commission from the ladies. They were away all day, and returned at night with the instruments, and with news that the house had been sacked by the cavalry, and part of it burned. That we had not noticed that fire at the time was perhaps because the flame it made must have been nearly in a line with the fire we had made ourselves.

In the course of the day there was assigned to a comrade and myself the pleasant duty of building beds upon which the women could pass the night comfortably. This was a pleasant duty, because it brought us near to these two ladies, and enabled us to see them and hear their voices; and for men who had been so long away from home, and from the sound of women's voices, this was a treat that others might not appreciate.

We made them good beds on a plan common in camp in those days. We went to the woods near and cut for each bed four stakes about four feet long, pointed at one end and crotched at the other, two straight rods five feet long, and six straight rods eight feet long.

The four pointed stakes, placed like the posts of an old-fashioned bedstead, were driven into the ground about a foot deep, with the crotches so turned as to hold evenly stout rods placed crosswise. Into these crotches were then rested the five-foot rods, and the eight-foot rods, placed lengthwise, were rested at each end on the cross-bars. These long rods were fastened at proper intervals with twine, and then were covered over nearly a foot deep with an even pad of short pine-twigs, carefully placed so that the stems should not protrude.

There is not a finer bed in the world than one so made. The long rods give just about the elasticity of a good bed-spring, and the comfort and fragrance of a mattress of pine-twigs would turn the head of a Sybarite.

Because the two women watched with so much attention our labors in this sphere of campaigning art, I thought it might also interest others to hear about it; hence the attention given to this trifle. But while they watched us they could not brood upon their own troubles, and any fact that turned their thoughts for a moment was perhaps welcome.

They overwhelmed us with an enthusiastic admiration of these contributions to their comfort. But we could not honestly accept all their compliments, for we had not invented this couch. It had grown in the camp somehow in the course of years, and we made it as we had seen others make it.

This was the first time I clearly saw Miss Phœbe Braxton.

She was a very handsome woman.

Her face was particularly fine. It was of a type sometimes seen in minature portraits of the beauties of a by-gone age; beauties who have left on ivory the scheme of their charms in colors dimmed by the touch of time, but whose names are gone forever, because the lips that loved to repeat them are dry as the tinder made from mummy.

In out-of-the-way regions these faces of the fine old type seem to linger; and it is as if the countenances of a breed of people formed themselves on the people's thoughts, and the modern thoughts had not yet reached these secluded spots to give a style of every-day vulgarity to the girls' faces.

Phœbe's face was the face of Pauline Bonaparte drawn in daintier lines, such as are characteristic of our climate—the same lines without the sensuous amplitude given by the blood of Corsica.

It was a long oval, finished above by gracefully disposed waves of raven hair which came almost to the eyebrows, and ended below by a chin as perfectly moulded as if it were the last result of nature's experience in that direction. The nose was not protrusive nor large, and yet its graceful length left no point to desire in that regard; and it filled with all the artistic effect required of any possible nose the space between the fine line of the eyebrows,—not arched, but perfectly straight,—and the beautiful curve of lips that pouted a little.

Her voice was very pleasant. There were some tones in it like the tones of a boy's voice; so that it was rather stronger and deeper than women's voices generally are. This had an odd effect at first, but grew upon you and proved a veritable charm; for never was a boy's voice so musical or so exquisitely modulated.

She had hazel eyes, with a softened, liquid, tender glance. She was a trifle tall, was slender, and perfectly graceful in every movement.

Altogether I do not believe I ever saw before so handsome and attractive a person.

She was shy to engage in conversation, though evidently eager to know the detail of all that had happened; but she left the pushing of these inquiries to the old lady, who exhibited an indomitable energy in that way.

Where was Dr. Braxton? Had anything happened to him? What had happened to the others? Were many hurt? Where was Willoughby? Who was killed? Where were we? Where were we going? What was to come next? These are but samples of the regular file-fire of questions she opened upon us and kept up.

My comrade, who was a cool fellow, with per-

6

haps just a trace of impudence in him, but with plenty
of good-nature,—his name was Sam Griffin,—said
in a calm, methodical way, when the old lady
called a halt:

"Now, ma'am, to begin at the beginning. Nearly as I recommember, your first question was,
'Where is Dr. Braxton?'"

"Yes," said the old lady, "that was very likely
my first question; he's my brother. He is this
lady's father."

"Oh, it's all right, ma'am; no harm in the question. Only, my pardner and me, we're pretty slow
about answerin' questions; and 'fore we had a
chance ter answer that one, you asked two or three
or four or five or six other ones, and the conversation kinder broke away, and I was tryin' to get it
into line again. And, as I said, I believe that question was on the right of the line."

"Well, it was, then. Where is Dr. Braxton?"

"Well, ma'am, he's in the guard-house."

"The guard-house! the guard-house!" And the
two ladies were filled with alarm and anxiety at
what this might mean.

"What had he done? Why was he locked up?
Would they murder him?"

Now, the word guard-house is generally more for-
midable than the fact. There is, as a rule, no house
in the case, as that word is commonly understood;
though if the word house means merely a place of
abode, this was as much a house as any other. Our
guard-house here, as in many other places, was

simply a marked-out limit of the ground we all slept upon. This limit was a square, inclosed on three sides by loose logs found near, and on the fourth side was the sentry. The prisoners could have stepped over the barriers at any point as easily as over a chalked line, but it was perfectly understood that to step over was death, unless permission was first given. Prisoners were not often refractory in that way.

It required a good deal of talking to convince the ladies that the guard-house was only one other innocent part of the mountain, and that keeping prisoners in it was only a military formality.

"Now," said Griffin, "if yer please, I'll go on with them questions. 'Was many hurt?' Well, not many, if you count in proportion to the whole company. But of eight that was engaged where the best fighting was done, seven was hit."

"Poor fellows!" said the young lady. "I hope they're not badly hurt."

"Well, ma'am," said Griffin, with a natural pathos in his voice, "there's some of them fellows for whom the war is over, and some for whom it is pretty nigh over."

"Heaven have pity on their mothers!" said the old lady.

"Yes, 'm," said Griffin, "that's, perhaps, mostly what'll be wanted in their families. But to go on. 'Where are we?' Yes, 'Where are we, and where are we going?' These is two questions that might as well be taken together. Nobody knows and nobody can find out."

"Lost in the mountain," said the old lady.

"Jist about the way of it," said the soldier.

"Well," said the old lady, "forty thousand men could be lost here and never find their way out."

"Which is a consoling observation," said Griffin.

Half the time she was in tears, and the younger woman now and again paid these tributes of sympathy to her aunt's trouble.

They were both exceedingly distressed at the news that the house was burned. But this fact seemed to fit happily into some conversation they had previously had, in which the young lady had maintained that they were now safer in our hands than they would be at their own home, with the country full of marauders, because regular troops under discipline are subject to restraint, while the "partisans" of Virginia were simply bandits who made patriotism their pretext.

Griffin, who was always full of stories, told them two or three things that had happened which seemed to prove this.

One serious observation the old lady made was that Major Pembroke did not come to see her, and she felt hurt at this want of attention.

But the young lady said:

"Aunty, dear, the officer had to give us all this distress on account of duty to his men, as Arthur told us; and now he is, no doubt, afraid you'll scold him as soon as you see him, and does not want to face it."

And I said, "I guess that's jist it, miss."

I thought it was very nice in this little woman to come to the Major's support in that ready way, and I liked her for it.

CHAPTER VIII.

It is possible to find a great many men in the world less satisfied with themselves and with their lot in life than we were in that camp. There was a good deal of glory in the air. We rejoiced in what seemed to us all a neat victory, and felt that we had shown ourselves equal to a difficult occasion in all the qualities that such an occasion calls for. This feeling would have lifted up our hearts against almost any hardship; but indeed we saw no hardship in that adventurous march through the mountains; for though the way was unknown, and our communications with the commissary department irremediably cut, we were not very hungry yet, and did not know the worst; and confidence and hope made us happy.

But there was one man in that camp thoroughly prostrated in the caves of despair. He had no part in our pride to sustain him, nor could the splendor of nature in that magnificent region make any impression whatever upon his fancy filled entirely with gloomy thoughts.

Willoughby was the most miserable man I ever saw. His exhilaration at one moment and his gloom at another were elements of his character; and he was now at the lowest curve of all possible mental depression.

And the Major also had at this time some hours of gloom.

The Major, when the surprise came upon us at night, and in all the subsequent endeavor, had dealt with it simply as the fact of the hour that had to be faced, however it might have been brought about; but he had, as soon as the enemy was evidently off our hands, given some thought to the effort to fathom the hidden history of the coming of the rebel cavalry, and to determine whether we owed any recognition on that score to any of the persons then in our camp.

Dr. Braxton, Mrs. Chichester, Miss Phœbe, Captain Willoughby—could any of these have done it? Could Willoughby have led us into a trap? Could the others have taken an unfair advantage of what seemed so much to please them? It was hard to believe either of these things; for to believe either was to lose some portion of the faith the Major had in all those pleasant people.

But he was not a man to hesitate between personal inclination and duty; and therefore there was a period of one day in which the life of Dr. Braxton was in imminent peril, and our relations with that family were likely to end in a tragedy that would have raised a great Southern cry against the barbarous spirit of Northern officers.

There was a certain old darky who pretended

to know positively that Dr. Braxton had sent intelligence through our lines that night; and all the other darkies declared with vociferous agreement not only that this was not true, but that this particular old darky had a special fame in all the country round for his qualifications as a liar.

Now, this testimony was divided with all the witnesses except one against that one; but it did not escape the Major that the crowd was declaring a negative,—was declaring that it did not know something,—and that one darky was declaring his positive knowledge of a definite fact.

But the observation that the old darky had a suspicious readiness to respond in any sort of questioning with the answer that he imagined would be agreeable to our side cast so much doubt upon his testimony that the Major saw he could not trust it; therefore he did not act.

Consequently the air was not cleared up, and the suspicion remained; and while he was still full of gloom upon this point, the Major called upon Willoughby in the guard-house. He could not have thought that Willoughby, even if he had any knowledge, would disclose it. He may have thought he could discover, at least, whether the other had a guilty knowledge that would make him shy of the object.

They were a gloomy pair. But Willoughby was so concentrated in his own gloom that he did not notice the Major's; while the Major, alert to notice the other's frame of mind, wondered whether this special depression was other than what might be expected in the circumstances.

"Blue-devils again?" he said.

"Yes," said Willoughby; "blue devils, and gray devils, and brown devils. My mind is a chaos of devils of all colors, every one worse than the other. In the other world or in this there can be no torture so bad as that of tormenting thoughts."

"Yes," said the Major; "I have some also."

"But at about daylight this morning I was gay enough," said Willoughby.

"Gay?" said the Major, with some wonder in his voice.

"Yes. You see, it was this way. I had made up my mind; I had determined what I would do. I had reached a desperate resolution. Concluding from all that has lately happened that association with me was a bane to all my friends, I had resolved to get out of this life; and the moment I had determined on that I was as calm and happy as ever I was before in all my days."

"But have you any weapon?"

"Not even a toothpick. But I had a plan. My intention was to run the guard, and to do it in a defiant way, so that the sentinel would have to fire; but to do it so clumsily that he could not possibly miss me."

"That was a good plan."

"And yet I was afraid it would fail."

"And if it had failed?"

"Then my intention was to return, overpower

the guardsman, and blow out my brains with his gun."

"Well, one way or the other would have made it certain, I should say. And yet this scheme that was the source of so much gayety you did not carry out?"

"No; and there again is my cursed ill-fortune. The evil one put into my head a fancy that a soldier has not a right to kill himself."

"An honest evil one, that."

"There came to me a thought that it is a soldier's duty to endure; and that for him to kill himself is in its way a kind of—well, desertion of the colors."

"Well, with that particular evil one I agree."

"And then, again,—my imagination is perhaps too active,—I could not get out of my thought the picture of these dear women with such an event added to their other troubles; and I cursed myself for an idiot. Fancy them with my corpse on their hands; and you know yourself how disagreeable fellows look when they are dead and yellow, especially without clean linen."

"Yes," said the Major. "In our regiment we always dress for battle."

"Now, Major, what could a fellow do in such circumstances? You are a cool one and have got more sense than I have. What would you do if you had concluded that life was not worth all this bother and trouble and turmoil, and yet felt that you could not honorably get out of it?"

"It seems to me," said the Major, "that your

question takes too many things for granted, because I do not believe I should ever reach your first conclusion unless I had a great deal more to bother me than there is to bother you."

"More!" said Willoughby. "Why, Major, just think of it, now; run over it with me. You know my personal mishaps of the first night of our acquaintance—I hardly count that. But consider the position of the ladies and the dear old doctor, either abandoned to the possibilities of the wilderness or compelled to move in the train of an enemy's force. The facts themselves as they stand are not so bad as the possibilities involved in case of any change. Your prosperity is their only safety, and you may be attacked again any night and your force perhaps overwhelmed, and what then? And but for me, for my idiocy, they would have been safe at home to day, for I brought all this trouble to their doors."

"Perhaps there is a divided responsibility," said the Major, coolly. "You brought my command there; but my command did no harm. It halted at night, and would have moved at daylight. But the person who brought the rebel cavalry there did worse. Who was that?"

Willoughby looked up with his open boyish air and said:

"I do not know."

"Whoever did that did all the mischief," said the Major. "Can you guess who did it?"

"No."

"Well, it was a foolish act to invite a battle about one's hearth-stone."

Thereupon Willoughby, caught by the words and the tone, looked anew at the Major, and their eyes met, and there was a silent conference in which each saw and felt that there was perfect fair-play in the other.

"Yes, Major," said Willoughby, "I know what troubles you, and the knowledge that it would trouble you has troubled me. But nobody in the circle about that hearth-stone invited that battle. They do not love your cause; but if they fight it, they will fight fair. If you suspect any person in Dr. Braxton's family of sending word through your lines, you do a great injustice."

Somehow the air was clearer after this declaration which did not argue anything, but only stated a conviction of the sincerity of which the Major was sure.

"Besides," said Willoughby, "why is it necessary to suspect any one? It did not happen that way. Did you ever hear what the old Arab said to the lion-hunter?"

"No."

"Well, he said—If in the wilderness you see a lion, and he seems not to see you, wait till he has passed on out of sight, and then turn short around and go the other way from that in which you were going when you saw him; because he saw you, and is going to wait for you at some convenient point in the direction in which you were moving."

"Well, I do not see any connection."

"What I would suggest is this. Several times yesterday on the march across the valley you saw bodies of partisans and kept your command hidden in the woods. They seemed not to see you. Some of them probably did see you, watched you, followed you, and reported your whereabouts to larger bodies, and so brought these down upon you at night."

"It may have happened that way," said the Major.

"It could not have happened any other way," said Willoughby; "but if there were a thousand ways in which it might have happened, none of them would have touched the honor of the Braxton family had they not been drawn into the circle of my evil destiny."

There was an interval of silence, and the Major said :

"If they are drawn into the circle of your destiny, you are drawn into the circle of theirs. Your life is associated with Phœbe's, let us say, as much as hers with yours; and is there not some selfish assumption in the fancy that if the superior powers have taken a hand in, they have interfered rather from your side than from hers ?"

"Why, perhaps there is," said Willoughby. "It did not strike me that way."

"Just imagine, now," said Pembroke, "a divine presence upon the earth like Phœbe Braxton: a beauty seldom equalled; a grace of demeanor and mind, and a silent sincerity and courage that rather realize what we conceive of goddesses than recall what we have seen in women. Just imagine all that, and then consider the absurdity of supposing that the heavenly forces would sway her destiny to suit that of fellows such as we are, and not ours to suit hers."

"Certainly, certainly," said Willoughby, a little dazed by new thoughts.

And then as they sat wordless again for a little while, and each mused on the path of his own speculations, Willoughby's thought of how his friends had been swept to calamity in the whirl of his ill-fortune gave place to a definite notion that Pembroke's admiration for Phœbe was somewhat enthusiastic; that Phœbe's beauty had impressed too much the mind of this fortunate enemy.

From this it was but a short step for a lover's fancy to the thought that Pembroke was in love with Phœbe; for how could he comprehend that any one could admire Phœbe and not feel toward her as he did?

At the moment Willoughby reached that point Pembroke had determined one that had floated vaguely in his own mind, and he said:

"Would it not be well to consider some way to get these ladies out of camp—some place to send them to—some plan by which they may be made safe against the chances of my company?"

"Perhaps it would," said Willoughby; but he said this with a less ready assent than might have been expected from one who could not but have been happy at the chance to get Phœbe away from the danger he now imagined.

For a perverse humor now suggested a wonder whether the Yankee officer—in a minute the friend of his romantic adventures had become a mere "Yankee officer"—had not some undeclared purpose behind his proposition. As the women were now, they had the guarantee of the honor of an officer under the constant observation of his men. Outside Pembroke's lines a few shots might remove Willoughby and the others. Nobody could ever tell who fired those shots, and Phœbe would be in the hands of her new admirer without even that thin defence.

Jealousy knows no limit in the extravagance of its apprehensions.

"Your thought that we might be assailed and overwhelmed any night," said Pembroke, "and the reflection of what might then happen to them, made me suppose that you would like to undertake to guide them to some safe place. You can be paroled to go for that purpose, if you care to, but I do not urge it."

"It is true," said Willoughby, "there is a possible danger here; but outside your lines evil is even more imminent. In this part of Virginia there is no government of law, and the men in arms, though they call themselves soldiers, are not always true to the name."

"You do not care, then, to make this effort?"

"No, sir."

"Well, then, I would suggest another step, also with a view to the welfare of these ladies. We are out of rations. Men whom we send out to forage either get lost in the wilderness or are captured; they never return.* We are on an uncertain run, and are at best so far from our destination that there is likely to be suffering from hunger before we reach it. Therefore I propose that you on parole leave the camp, alone, and endeavor to help us; that if you find a farm-house you send food for the women; always with the understanding that if you find Union troops you report us, with the guarantee of your parole, and if you fall into the hands of Southern troops you are free, but must keep our secret, while doing all that you may in honor to help the Braxtons."

Only one thought went through Willoughby's mind as he heard this out, and that was:

"He is determined to get rid of me, one way or another."

Pembroke was surprised at Willoughby's indifference to this proposition, and did not know what to make of it; and when Willoughby said that he "would like to think it over," Pembroke left him, with the conviction that there was something in him that he did not understand.

From that interview the Major went and called

---

*We had lost in this way at that time seven privates, a sergeant, and a corporal.

upon the ladies. His mind was easy about the Braxtons as to the point at least that had been in it when he first sat down with Willoughby, and some reaction provoked the notion that he had done them injustice, and he wished now to make such reparation as there might be in courteous attention.

Every daughter of Eve has, I suppose, enough of the feminine instinct to put up a hand and feel if her hair is properly adjusted as she suddenly finds herself in the presence of a man; perhaps, even, every woman has enough coquetry to want to produce a good effect upon any man she meets—for is not that the designated purpose of her charms? It is therefore not a point of great consequence that nobody ever saw Phœbe in our camp but her toilet was as scrupulously and daintily made as the Major's own, and he was one of the men who indulged himself to an extreme degree in that piece of military foppery of wanting to be always ready to die in clean linen and with his hair parted.

It must have had some peculiar effect upon the Major that afternoon to find Phœbe so resplendently beautiful in the simplicity of her toilet; for his call was very short. Some agitation interfered with his enjoyment of that pleasant company, and soon after he had left them Mrs. Chichester and Phœbe came forth and also made a call upon Willoughby. They talked very earnestly for many minutes; they talked of the project of their all leaving the camp together, and Phœbe was against it; they talked of Willoughby's going alone, and Phœbe was

7

in favor of it, whereupon Willoughby became obstinately silent. Then Mrs. Chichester walked away a little, but Phœbe stayed with Willoughby.

Willoughby spoke suddenly and rapidly.

"The Yankee Major," he said with the irritation and half-anger of a jealous man, and watching her as if he spoke rather to see the effect his words would have than merely to convey a thought, "the Major wishes that you may love him."

"He is not so foolish," she said with a perfectly natural air. "How can he imagine that I should love two men at once? But he has not by word or otherwise treated me in any way but with the most distant and respectful courtesy."

"Ah, he is an adroit one. He would not go beyond cool courtesy unless certain that a more familiar style would be welcome."

"Well, if he waits to adopt a more familiar style until he shall see in my conduct some evidence that it would be welcome, he will wait at least as long as you, Arthur, can desire."

"You can scarcely comprehend what precautions may be necessary with such a man."

"He is a man of honor, Arthur."

"I wish you had never seen him, Phœbe."

"It was not my fault that I saw him."

"You reproach me for doing what I was tempted to do by the desire to see you."

"I do not reproach you; but if I did, it would be because, having brought me into such relations, your own faith is the first to fail."

And thus were Arthur and Phœbe fairly started down the incline of that dangerous indulgence, a lover's quarrel.

We got away from that camp at nightfall, intending to make five miles and rest; one of the principal points involved in this short march being that it was high time we changed our position, because it might have been studied by some one for a night-attack; and once on foot to get away from that possibility, it did not seem worth while to move less than five miles. We cut loose from all the darkies except those we could make use of as guides, and the women went with us because they were afraid to be left in this wild region alone, and the Major felt himself responsible for their welfare.

We made our five miles that night, and made twenty the next day. Half-rations was all we had now, and moving in this stony wilderness of the mountain-top, we had not seen a house nor an ear of corn. Some of the men got two little thin sheep on the second day's march, the little remnants perhaps of some larger number that had been driven away to feed the enemy. At the end of our twenty-five miles we called the place "Camp Hungry Man's Home." From that camp the Major sent out next day ten men to skyugle through the whole region for supplies and information. We never saw any of those men again, though we did not march for a day. At peep of day we were on foot again. This was the sixth day from the time we had left Brax-

ton House, and we had lived all this time on the
rations that Lieutenant Wood had hastily packed on
our four mules that night. But we had now reached
the head of the ridge or spur we were on, and were
descending from the mountain somewhat on the
western slope. The darkies said we were making
for Winchester. We estimated that day's march at
ten miles.

We halted at a place the darkies called Corkscrew
Cut, though why they did not know.

It was a queer place. All one side was covered
by the perpendicular rocky wall of mountain at the
foot of which we stood and from which sloped out
a wide and pleasant plateau. The edge of this plateau was the brow of another steep descent, as if the
mountain went down in natural terraces or great
steps. But we had come into this place at one end,
and the way down the mountain was at the other
end, for we were yet far above the level of the
valley.

We were now at a critical point in our progress.
If we stayed on the mountain, we should all starve to
death; if we went down, we might march into the
enemy's lines, for we could only guess at the possibility of movements of troops that had taken place
in those days. But the boys were used to such
critical possibilities, and they did not lie awake
thinking about our position. Neither, I suppose,
did the ladies, because to march into a town held
by the enemy's troops could not especially distress
them.

CHAPTER IX.

In the afternoon of the day we spent in Corkscrew Cut Major Pembroke invited the ladies and the prisoners to dine with him on the parade, and the boys who had charge of the headquarters mess had a lively time getting ready for that little feast. It is never very easy to prepare a banquet in time of famine, but the effort stimulates imagination, and that day the boys actually found a lean heifer somewhere on the mountain-side.

The point of this little spree was the proposed departure of Willoughby; for it appears that he had that day reconsidered his refusal, and sent word to the Major that he would willingly try his fortune as a scout in the valley.

Some of the boys joked between themselves about the Major's attentiveness to the ladies. They thought his heart was, maybe, caught in the glances of Miss Phœbe's beautiful eyes. And as the Major was an extremely handsome man and a man of the most engaging and amiable manners, it was thought to be rather unfortunate for Captain Willoughby that his fair sweetheart had fallen into such pleasant company.

My own opinion at that time was that the Major's eyes had more effect upon Miss Braxton than hers upon him. He could not but have admired her. I would defy any man in that respect. Neither could any man have failed to react with all his sympathies to the case of a refined and charming little lady suddenly dragged out from the dainty and maidenly reserve of her home life, and rushed through such a rough bit of campaigning experience, living in camp with a pretty tough crowd of soldiers, carried through the edge of a hard mountain-fight at the first start, and so doubtful of the future that she contemplated with terror the moment when she should be parted from all these rough enemies.

Therefore the Major may have felt tenderly toward her, and no doubt did; but it seemed to me, from the moment that I saw Miss Phœbe after the Major called upon the ladies for the first time in "Camp Git-away," that there was a difference in her. Some change had come over the little lady's life; and I have always thought that in that little half-hour when the Major had chatted with Phœbe and her old aunty together, and tried perhaps to excuse himself from the accusation of any presumed want of gallantry, then and there, the dear little woman had fallen in love with that fine, courteous and gallant gentleman.

She in all probability did not know it; and if anybody had spoken to this effect, she would have resented what the observation might imply as to frivolity in her affections. But the case was clear to me, and I certainly did not blame her. Willoughby was no doubt a pleasant, good-looking fellow, but not a man to be mentioned on the same day with the Major. And though when a woman loves a man I suppose she sees him in a very different light from that in which he appears to others, yet I doubt if a woman could ever get her senses so over-whelmed in that kind of delusion as not to note the contrast between two such men, especially if she be placed with regard to them as Miss Braxton was in our camp.

As the boys talked this over they kept on with their preparations. We had found near by a lumber-man's shed, which we had used for kindling-wood, all but the door, and out of that we made a table, supported upon stakes driven into the ground. For seats the ladies had cracker-boxes, and the others had the pads of the mule-harness with coats thrown over.

Our polished tin cups and our knives and forks gave the table the appearance of a bric-à-brac deal-er's lay-out.

There was a beefsteak for the grand dish. It was cooked by one of our fellows who could broil meat over any smoky fire and without a gridiron— a thing that every one can't do. His plan was to have the pan very hot and very dry,—that is, no grease in it,—and to put the steak in then, and turn it often; the outside burned into a little crust and kept the juice in.

It was a bright company, but they were a little

awkward when they first sat down. The old lady, however, soon got them over that.

"Major Pembroke," she said, "there is one thing in regard to your house here on the mountain that I like very much. You have no rats."

At this sally there was a general laugh of pleasant surprise.

"Yes," she went on, "it is a great advantage. At Braxton we are overrun with them, and they are a dreadful plague. You can scarcely understand, I suppose, what a comfort it is, when you happen to wake in the night, not to hear those mischievous creatures rattling up and down in the wall or gnawing at the beams."

"Well," said the Major, "we are delighted to know that our hospitality is not entirely without its agreeable side. I hope that Miss Braxton has also found something that may lighten in her thoughts its rougher features."

"Yes," she said, "I also have found at least one good point in your house; it is not lonesome."

As she said this with a ladylike tranquillity, acquitting herself of an obligation to which she had been challenged, her eyes turned softly and confidently toward Willoughby, and that poor fellow imagined he was the object of the pleasant thought behind this observation. But I saw that he was not, and I believe that old Aunt Hetty saw it also. For the glance at Willoughby was full of the confidence that a girl has toward a fellow of little moment; but the timidity with which she tried to keep her eyes away from those of Pembroke's and the nervous uneasiness which she could not control told another story.

"Well, ladies and gentlemen," said Lieutenant Wood, "upon me honor it is not altogether the worst house we ever were in; far from it, indeed, especially when we consider the presence of the ladies, and the honor they do to our table. But there is one pynt in respect to which I would be glad to change many a house like this against one like Braxton House. We have none of the docthor's foine old Medayrah."

Hereupon the doctor and the lieutenant dropped into a pleasant consideration of the merits of the different kinds of Madeira, and the thoughts thus excited may have flavored the simple beverage the boys had brought them.

Although there was an evident effort to be cheery over that feast, it dragged a little, for all but Willoughby; since the ladies and the old doctor, who knew of Willoughby's departure, could not but feel uncertain of the issue, though it was their best hope for a happy end to an enforced adventure. But Willoughby himself was almost unnaturally gay. This may have been another exhibition of that peculiarity of his character to which he had referred when he told the Major how happy he was when he had made up his mind to kill himself. Doubts and uncertainties were the only things that overwhelmed him. In the face of any certainty, however bad, he could be gay. Thus

having concluded to leave the camp as the Major
had proposed, he had suddenly become the most
cheerful one of the company, and laughed with a
light heart, and quoted Shakspeare.

One quotation he made seemed so apt that old
Braxton thanked him for it, and said the words
comforted him.   It was:

> " All places that the eye of Heaven visits
>   Are to a wise man ports and happy havens."

Nobody lingered at table, therefore, and as it
was determined that Willoughby should start at
once, while there was yet a bit of daylight, he was
accompanied on his way by all those who had supped with him.   But the Major and Lieutenant Wood
only went about twenty yards beyond our pickets;
while the ladies and the doctor went a good way
farther, and did not return until the Major had begun to feel a little uneasy about them.

Willoughby went ahead upon his adventure as
cheerily, perhaps, aside from his hysterical gayety,
as any other man could possibly have gone with the
same incentives at once to go and to stay.

He had his freedom in his hands, but in the circumstances he probably did not set an extravagant
value upon it; and what gallant young fellow leaving his lady-love in the hands of his enemies, exposed to all the frowns and caprices of Step-mother
Fortune, would have valued more highly than he did
this singular negative that we have deified with the

name of freedom—this mere absence of restraint
upon one's will?

Willoughby's recent experiences had taught him
the wisdom of a careful advance in any region which
might be held by troops; so that from the moment
he left the camp, even on the rugged rocky crest of
the hill, he was attentive to every sight and sound.
In that spirit he went on until he gained the line of
heavy timber half way down the mountain; and
through the dim grand aisles of the woodland—
aisles whose arches were pillared by oaks and chestnuts of a century's growth—he kept his way in the
same spirit, startled many a time by the scurry of
the squirrel and the scream of the jay, but finding
ever that his solitude was complete as to humanity.

He had avoided every opportunity to get immediately down into the valley by old wood-roads or
neighborhood paths, because these are generally
through a somewhat open region, and he appre-
hended that if he approached any spot in the possession of either our men or the enemy, he would
be seen as soon as he saw, and might not be able to
get away even if he chose. Consequently he lost a
great deal of time in keeping along the wooded
brow of the mountain for many a mile to find a spot
from which he could study the valley before going
down to it.

He found at last an apparently satisfactory place.
There was a sort of arm of the mountain-land, a
kind of wooded promontory which ran out into the
valley almost at a right angle with the general direc-

tion of the ridge, and from which he rightly judged
he could get a view above and below of the open
region, while it was probable that a road skirted at
its extremity the foot of this high point.

But here he found the same difficulty that he had
found all along the side of the main ridge: it was
easier to scan the far, far-away parts of the valley than
to inspect parts nearer by, because the whole slope
here also was timbered, and at any point he might
place himself his view was intercepted by the tops
of trees whose roots were thirty or forty or even a
hundred feet below him. He was sure, however,
that sooner or later he would find an open place
from which he could get a good lookout, and so he
continued his tramp. But now he began to hear
familiar noises; first a far-away bugle-call came so
faintly, yet so naturally, that it hardly attracted his
attention, for at that moment he was critically considering in his inmost thought whether it was because Phœbe's eyebrows were in line with one
another and made almost two parts of a straight line
that her forehead had so fine an effect, and why
nature had not made all women's eyebrows that
way.

But the distant bugle-call was repeated, and there
was a far-away screaming of hungry mules; and one
sound following another, it suddenly dawned upon
the Captain's mind, with all the effect of a grand
discovery, that the air about him was filled with the
noises of an army encamped or on the march.

What army was it?

If it was a Southern army, did he want to make himself known, return to his duty, and leave Phœbe in the mountains in such circumstances? If it was a Northern army, what was best to be done?

But he must first ascertain what army it was, and ascertain quickly, because there was not a great deal of daylight left.

In the hope to get a glimpse of what was going on in the direction from which these sounds came, and perhaps to be able to see enough to solve the doubt as to what troops they were he heard, the Captain conceived the notion of surveying the scene from the branches of one of the tall trees about him. If one is already on the side of a mountain he is not, to be sure, a great deal higher for being at the top of a tree, but that little elevation of thirty or forty feet puts him above the surrounding obstacle of the foliage of other trees; and in fact a tree top was a very common site for a signal-station with the armies on both sides.

He selected his tree in a little while—a tall, enormous chestnut which stood just at the outermost point of the promontory. As the mountain-side fell away somewhat steeply at that place, the top of this tree stood out in the forest almost as a church-steeple does in a landscape; yet from the ground at the root of this tree the view of the valley was entirely shut out by the tops of the trees that grew on the downward slope.

Now the stem of this patriarch of the woods stood like a doric column, straight and smooth for thirty feet without a branch, and larger about than the bulge of a large barrel.

Consequently to mount into the branches of this tree by climbing its own stem in the usual way was not possible, for no human arms could grasp it with "purchase" enough to sustain a man's weight; but the problem thus presented of how to get up had been solved by the superabundant readiness of prolific Nature, who might almost be supposed to have imagined that such a need would arise.

Within the space shaded by the branches of the chestnut several smaller trees had sprouted, but had not flourished. They maintained a doubtful existence in the shadow of the giant, as small traders do in the presence of some great monopolist. They were nature's reserve of recruits, ready to fill the place of the veteran when he should go down in some tremendous battle of the November elements. In this second line of the forest army one tree was more vigorous than the others, and had pushed his way to the sunshine, sending a straight stem far up between the branches of the senior. This was a thrifty oak of ten summers whose stem was just of convenient size for climbing, and whose rough coat was a help to the climber, while above the stem of the oak was against one of the main branches of the chestnut.

Up this smaller tree Captain Willoughby went with comparative ease and celerity, and reaching the branch against which it grew, made his way along that to a point on the chestnut from which he had a good lookout, and could see all that was then to be seen in the valley.

But this was not a great deal, for the night had come as suddenly as if a curtain were drawn. Here and there in the landscape he could see a fire like the bivouac-fire of troops halted for the night; he could hear also the far-away murmur of moving regiments and wagons, but could get no definite information from any of these facts.

He had had his climb for nothing; but no, not entirely for nothing, because he now made one pleasant discovery.

In some early calamity of its life this old chestnut had lost the upper part of its main stem, which had been broken away at that very point at which the large main branches started out. Consequently these main branches were disposed like the frame of a crib, and the space between was a roomy hollow filled just now with an inviting bed of leaves, the leaves of many summers, perhaps, which had gathered and decayed there year after year. The Captain perceived in this a good halting-place, and a not uncomfortable one in which to pass the night.

Willoughby congratulated himself upon the good fortune of this discovery, as he snuggled down in this happy hollow with the satisfaction of one who is weary at once with worry and with bodily fatigue.

His muscles were worn with his day's march; his mind was worn with anxiety as to the chances of his present attempt; and he felt that the way would seem clearer to him for some hours of sleep.

How delicious is the languor with which we "turn in" away from the world, from doubts, uncertainties, dangers, discomforts, in such a moment!

Not a squirrel on the branches could be safer from the scrutiny of any chance stranger who might pass below than he was, and at the first peep of day he would be able to see just what he might venture in the valley.

In a few minutes the drowsy charm came over his senses, but he did not immediately fall into a sound sleep. He was perhaps rather too weary for that, and in his restlessness worked himself deeper into his soft bed, and found it all the pleasanter for this. He did not notice, however, that his feet had worked their way into what seemed a free place, had in fact been forced through the loose tissue of leaves that constituted his bed; for these leaves matted together only in decay did not afford a great deal of resistance, and the feet of the sleeper were actually hanging through his mattress in an undefined hollow of the tree below him. He did not notice this as he turned over once more in his first uneasy sleep; but that turn broke a way for his whole body through the mattress of leaves, and then—

He was startled as one who dreams he has fallen over a precipice; but, crushed, bruised, hurt, and left unconscious, he did not awaken to know that it was only a dream.

As soon as he gathered his wits together a little, his first thought was that he had fallen from the tree and was lying bruised at the bottom, or among

the broken, craggy stones down the side of the hill.
But how was it then that he could not stir; that
he could scarcely breathe; that his arms, straight
out above his head, were held there by some inde-
finable force, so that he could not move them; that
he could not bend his body nor lift a foot?

Was it a dream, and was this some horrible nightmare?

Alas, no! Captain Willoughby was lodged-in the
hollow of the old chestnut, far down near to its
roots. His bed of leaves had been only a deceptive
cover to this dreadful trap, for the straight, enormous stem of the tree was only a monstrous tube,
like a great organ-pipe, and into this tube, his body
falling from on high, and driven by its own weight,
was forced to the end, and there held as closely almost as if he had been built into a wall of solid
masonry.

There we shall leave him for the present, vaguely
wondering whether the tough sapwood that bound
him in was the wood of his coffin, but gamely ad-
dressing his reasoning faculties to that grand but
common human problem, how to get out of the hole
into which a malign destiny had dropped him.

8

CHAPTER X.

THAT evening we had a parade on the level plateau, and turned out in good shape what was left of the company—about twenty-two boys that had fought at Yorktown, Williamsburg, Fair Oaks, Savage Station, Frazer's Farm, and Malvern Hills.

The two ladies and the old doctor came out to see the show, and when the parade was over they and the Major enjoyed a promenade to and fro across the front of the plateau, which was so much like the battlement of an ancient fortress that an old-time chevalier or feudal lord might have felt at home there.

In all my marches I never saw such a sunset as we saw that day. For two days the weather had been dry and breezy; and though the air was fresh and still, it was summer air, and it gave one an ecstatic pleasure to breathe it and live in it. Below us spread that wonderful piece of country, the Shenandoah Valley, more beautiful, I am sure, than any Garden of Eden ever was; and behind the farther wall of that valley the sun went down red fierce and slow like a giant at bay, disputing his ground by inches, and filling the heavens with the glory of his battle.

It was no wonder, therefore, that the Major and the ladies enjoyed this promenade.

Presently, however, the doctor and the old lady grew weary, and sat down at one end of this reach of promenade; but the Major and the fair Phœbe kept on, and entertained one another with the pleasant interchange of ideas that may flow from such circumstances.

At this time I was on post as sentinel at the upper end of the plateau, and as their promenade when they came that way reached to within a few feet of where I paced my beat, I caught from time to time, and in a fragmentary way, a little of what they said; and I listened, not to hear the words, but only to hear the witchery of that woman's voice; yet the words came to me, of course.

All that I heard them say ran, strangely enough, upon one subject, and a pleasant subject, for it was provoked by the word Cupid, and touched upon the figurative representations of the passion of love. Perhaps that is not an unnatural theme between a gentleman and a lady who do not feel so deeply interested in one another but that they may treat this passion in a tone of pleasant raillery and laugh at the little god as an impostor and as one who fools others.

But the tone of frivolity was all on the Major's side. The lady's words were convincingly serious. She clearly did not regard love as a joke.

"That a passion should be pictured as a god," said Pembroke, "implies the sovereignty of passion."

"No," said the lady, "it implies that this passion is pure, disinterested, and absolute in its dominion over the human soul."

And then they passed down to the other end of the promenade and I did not hear; but they apparently kept to the same point, for as they came again I heard the Major say:

"And yet under the influence of this dominion see what happens to every one, nearly. What a mad intoxication it becomes! How duty and great obligations are forgotten while men linger in the enjoyment of delights which make one imagine that the story of the garden of Armida is the most real picture of existence."

"But," said the siren-voice, "is not this perhaps intended to teach us that our duties and obligations so called are merely conventionalities, to which in a perverted imagination we give an importance that they do not deserve? Is it not nature's testimony that in the struggle to succeed in life we have taken an erroneous measure of what is important, and that the fruits of this passion are worthier than the things that most men pursue?"

Then it seemed to me there was silence in heaven for half an hour more or less, and they made two or three turns in which I did not hear a word. Next time there was more of the light raillery.

"And this little god," said the Major, "carries a torch to set the world aflame with."

"No," said the lady, "I should understand that he carries a torch in order that those under his dominion may see life in the light he casts upon it, rather than in the changeable light of common day."

It seemed to me that at that moment the world about these two was illumined by that peculiar radiance, and that the mystic glimmer of the stars was not in conflict with it.

They walked on, and the conversation assumed a different tone.

"In one way or another," said the Major, "we are near to the end of an association that misfortune has inflicted upon you."

"Oh, Major Pembroke," said Miss Braxton, "please say it in some other way; for while it is a misfortune, of course,—especially to Arthur and Aunty and Papa,—yet there are other ways in which we will more delight to remember much of all this."

"Well," he continued, "I only wanted to say that it is well to reflect upon the possibilities before us, that we may be the more ready for whatever comes, and therefore—"

"And yet," she said, interrupting, "I thought that with the many incommodities of a soldier's life there was mingled the one charm of carelessness for the future, and that freedom from bother which is found in taking things as they come."

"Well," said the Major, "that is rather an ideal account of it than a true statement of experience in our army. Where can you imagine more anxiety involved than in the thought of a lost battle or a lost opportunity? And then if one happens to be responsible for the immediate safety of fair ladies—"

"Yes, yes," she said; "but if we are to part so soon, that will be over, and I hope you will not remember it too severely against us."

"Come what may," he said, "I shall always hold it as the happiest chance of my life that I met you."

And she made a little courtesy as in a merry mockceremony; but the words pleased her.

"We are now," said the Major seriously, "not more than a march from some town or village in the valley, and from that point we shall get to Winchester as we are, or perhaps as prisoners. I shall wait here to-morrow in hope to hear from Captain Willoughby, and then go on, as advised by him or without his advice; for if he does not return or send, it will be a sign in itself."

"A sign of what?" she said.

"A sign that he has fallen into Confederate hands, would not betray me, and could not send help without."

"Yes," she said; "or perhaps a sign of some new misfortune. Arthur is wonderfully unlucky."

"Not in one respect, at least," said the Major.

But I heard no more of that conversation, though it appeared to continue; for I was relieved and went to my quarters, where I heard the boys discussing the manœuvre of sending Willoughby out as a scout.

Strangely enough there was a sense of relieved tension; a feeling of lightness of spirit such as old soldiers experience at the beginning of a battle, because they comprehend that the puzzle and labor of marching and manœuvring and all the uncertainty are over and things are to be determined one way or another forthwith.

This was due to the universal prevalence of the opinion that Willoughby would betray us, and that there would be high jinks before we were all a day older.

He was, if we never saw him again, only a prisoner gone, and in that sense no great loss; departure made one less mouth to feed, and he might be of service to us as to supplies and other assistance.

All this was clear enough, and as clearly admitted; yet there were many who did not like this departure.

Some had no other reason except simply that "they did not like it." They perhaps had some instinctive perception of possible evil consequences, but could not define it.

Others, bolder or more equal to the occasion in speech, put it clearly that "you can't trust one of those fellows in any circumstances." They did not believe that an enemy could possibly find himself possessed of an advantage without using it. Consequently they argued that Willoughby's departure meant trouble for us—the destruction or capture of what was left of the company through his betrayal of our position to the enemy; and many a fellow lay down in our camp that night in the absolute conviction that he would be awakened to rally for the last desperate fight that Company H would ever be called upon to face.

My remembrance of the last waking hours of that ever-memorable day is distinctly with me yet. Our mess was around a little fire, and the boys had eaten their supper and lighted their pipes, and were talking over Willoughby's departure and a hundred other things more or less related to our position. Wrapped in my blanket, and stretched on the cool earth a dozen feet away, I fell into that edge of dreamland where one feels half the charm of slumber, yet has a waking consciousness of all that is going on.

As I lay that way, watching the faces of the boys illumined by the little blaze of the camp-fire,—a pretty picture framed in the infinite glory of the night,—I heard the clear, fine voice of Charley Otis recite a poem that our fellows had a great liking for, and that had been written by one of our company. It was called "We've Come to Stay," and was as follows:

> "They were not pranked for dress parade;
>   They wore no plumes; no golden braid
>   Glistened or gleamed with lustre gay
>   On those who through the tangled vines
>   Called with a jibe across the lines,
>   'Heigh, Johnnie Reb, we've come to stay!'

> "From Malvern Hills to Roanoke,
>   In rain and shine and battle-smoke,
>   Always alert and always gay;
>   In march by night, and fight at dawn,
>   On many a field their line was drawn:
>   And where 'twas drawn, 'twas drawn to stay.

" Behind that line that could not yield
  No rebel footstep touched the field
      On which our battle-rainbow rose;
  Behind that line of fire and steel
  The dead might fall, the dying reel,—
      But only dead or dying foes.

" Ah me! too true that battle-cry
  Echoed to hearts then proud and high;
      And many a grave beside the way,
  On mountain-height, by vale and stream,
  Or where the woodlands drowse and dream,
      Will well attest they went to stay.

' There they yet stand as daylight falls,
  Still sentinels on freedom's walls;
      And shall stand till the final day.
  And when his bugle-call divine,
  Gabriel shall sound along the line,
      They'll answer, ' Here! We came to stay.' "

And then another fellow gave a song in a gayer
note. It was a jingle the boys loved to hear, and
they called it " The Fringe of Steel."

"Forward! Forward! Forward!
    And bugles far and fine
  Send the brave order right and left,
    And onward sweeps the line!
  And every soldier's ready
    And proudly fills his place;
  For now at last the foe is here,
    And we are face to face.

' Across the open broken ground,
    Breast-high the river through,
  And bravely up the other slope
    Goes on the line of blue.

What though some heroes here and there
    The deadly reason feel?
The azure line sweeps grandly on,
    Bearing its fringe of steel!

"And now the air above them
    Is filled with bursts of foam,
And many an iron messenger
    Reaches his destined home;
And cannons play their grape-shot
    As summer clouds play rain,
And the close file-fire wakens death,
    But all alike in vain!

"For, see, the levelled pieces
    In the last mortal brunt,
Right at the muzzles of the guns,
    Carry the fringe in front!
Forward!   Forward!   Forward!
    And bugles far and fine
Send the brave order wide and free,
    And onward goes the line!"

And thus hearing the songs and stories and gabble of the boys about the fire, I drowsed away and
lost myself in slumber.

CHAPTER XI.

As nearly as I can count an hour by recollection of the incidents of the night, it was at about two A.M., when all seemed as peaceful in our little camp as the night may be in a city of the dead, that the report of a rifle-shot rang out and rattled and reverberated up the hills. Every man in camp was on foot in an instant. Sometimes it is true a rifle is discharged by accident, even in the night; sometimes a nervous soldier on picket-duty will fire at what he only imagines is a man. But everybody instinctively felt that there was no accident this time. Every one jumped to the conclusion that they who had suspected the Confederate officer were right; that he had betrayed our secret, and that the enemy was upon us.

That shot was fired at the line of our picket down the hill; but there was scarcely time to have a doubt as to its whereabouts before another shot settled it, and then we heard it bang! bang! bang! all up and down that very short line, as when the pickets all descry the same object and blaze away at it as fast as they can load and fire. Our line was drawn up, in shorter time than it takes to tell it, across that narrow part of the plateau from which a kind of blind wood-road led down the hill; and as we silently loaded our pieces, we could hear the shout and rush of a conflict up the hillside, and knew that the enemy were on our fellows, and that all would come in together.

But that could not be helped, and we stood at ready to receive them with at least one good fire, and with the confidence that we could give them all they came for unless there was enough of them to sweep around our line, which did not cover half the width of the plateau.

"Take care to fire above our boys as they come in," said the Major.

And the brilliant gleam of the stars would easily help us to that end.

In another second came the rush, the tumble, the flight, the pursuit, helter-skelter, pell-mell, of a mass of horsemen driving our fellows; and just as they came up the slope fair on a level, the Major's voice rang over the din, clear and loud:

"Fire!"

We fired like one man; and then the front rank at the order fixed bayonets, went forward a pace, and dropped to receive cavalry, while we behind pegged away at the mass. Our first fire of about fourteen rifles staggered them, or perhaps knocked the head of their column into a cocked hat, for there was a moment's lull in the noise; and there was a gleam of hope that if some of them did not scramble down to our left and find the end of the line we might beat them off.

But it was only a gleam. There were a great many behind those who first came, and they were not the sort of fellows we had had on our hands at Braxton House, but regular cavalry from a North Carolina regiment; and though astonished at our first fire, they swept in an instant later and filled the whole plateau, and rode us down front and rear. There was a desperate conflict of four or five minutes, when our line was broken. Sabres and bayonets encountered with the fine jingle of such metal; clubbed muskets and carabines came down on men's heads; there were shouts and groans and curses,— and Company H was done for. Every man of our little party was either dead or wounded. It was the most complete calamity I ever saw.

Exactly how long a time elapsed I don't know, nor what was the occasion of the delay; for, dazed and hurt, I had almost lost the power of observation or reflection; but after a while I heard near me an officer report to him who was the commander of this cavalry that this

"Seemed to be Yankee soldiers from east of the mountain; that there were twenty-four; that the officers were killed or mortally wounded; that there were twelve men dead of the Yankees, and fifteen of their own; that all the remainder of the Yankees were hurt, and that ten of their own men were too badly hurt to go on."

"They fought like the deuce, Charley," said the commander as he sat sidewise on his horse and smoked a pipe, "for such a little party."

"Yes, sir; they were tough fellows."

"They must be from the Army of the Potomac."

"Well, sir, they wasn't militia."

"It's singular they should be here. Hi, there! send word to the captain of the right company to keep a sharp lookout ahead; there must be more, certainly. And, Charley, leave the dead and mortally wounded where they are, but take half a dozen files and send the other wounded with our wounded down the mountain."

This order rather surprised me; but I could not then give myself any account of why it should surprise me.

Then in a little while I heard the movements of this force like the rush of a storm; and certainly it had come upon us like a mounted whirlwind, as it moved away over the mountain in the direction from which we had reached this accursed spot. The order which I had heard given with regard to us was acted upon so energetically that by daylight we were all in the street of some little village near the foot of the mountain, the wounded rebs sharing with us the refreshment of the cups of coffee they made by the roadside.

Some of our boys, as we went down the mountain, talked about the fight in that spirit of free criticism of the officers that was perhaps too common in our army. Many wondered whether it would have been possible for us to whip the cavalry if we had been differently handled, and thought that a small body of infantry like ours should be equal to a regiment of cavalry on such a hillside. That might be true as to some hillsides; but on this succession of easy slopes the cavalry was not at a great disadvantage.

One fellow thought we could have done better if we had been spread through the woods, flanking the road by which the cavalry advanced, and had thence peppered them with skirmish-fire.

Another thought we would have been posted that way if we had not been surprised.

"Well," said the first, "what right has a company of a veteran regiment to be surprised, anyhow?"

In short, there was the usual array of military knowledge; but a generous silence about the Major, which would not have been observed if he had not perished in the conflict.

In my opinion, infantry can never hold its ground against cavalry in such a case; that is, if there is plenty of cavalry, and the cavalry knows what it wants to do, and is determined to do it. Plenty of stories I know are told about adamantine squares, and all that; but a good deal of it is romance, and the rest is nonsense. Suppose only one horseman comes, and you put a dozen bullets into his nag and two or three into him, and have got a line of bayonets ready. He jumps his horse fair into your square just as he's two or three paces away. You kill 'em both, of course, but horse and man fall on your line. The mere dead weight of the horse's body, not to mention his struggling as he kicks and sprawls, opens two or three files. Half a dozen other horsemen follow at that point, and your square is gone.

That's the way it seems to me, though we never had much of that. As for those squares of the Old Guard at Waterloo which are always quoted, I don't believe the story. It is a romantic exaggeration to glorify a little more the subjects of a fine old legend. Perhaps the cavalry had other fish to fry just then, and could not attend to those old duffers. Perhaps it was the correct tactical thing in that battle to leave the squares alone, and go for the fellows that were on the run. Either that, or it was not first-rate cavalry.

Commonly every cavalryman is ready to let another cavalryman have the glory of being the first man in the square, and that sort of generosity saves the square.

One of our fellows exhibited all the way down the hill a great deal of distress for a reason that seemed rather comic to the rest of us.

"Imagine it!" he said, "what a name for a fight—Corkscrew Cut! Why, when it appears in the reports that our company fought till the last man was down at Corkscrew Cut, the boys will only laugh. All the glory will be lost in the thought of such a ridiculous name;" and thereupon he launched out into a tirade against the absurdity of Southern names, and the commonplace character of the names of our battles by comparison with the names of the fights in the ancient wars.

But another one of the fellows, a college man, used him up on that point about the ancient names, though he agreed with him that it was disgusting to be killed or wounded at a place with such a name as Corkscrew Cut.

"As for the ancient names," said this fellow, "they were just like our names, often only descriptions of natural facts—combinations of familiar syllables; but they have a dignity for us due to their association with great events rather than with mere incident of topography. Thermopylæ, for instance, means the pass at the hot springs; but such a phrase as the fight at Hot Springs Pass will never get at the roots of your hair as do those wonderful words, the fight at Thermopylæ."

In the village we learned that General Pope had been pulverized on the eastern side of the mountains a few days before; that all of Lee's army was sweeping into Maryland and Pennsylvania; and that it would be at Philadelphia in a few days, as the Army of the Potomac was cut to pieces.

That was their story.

Down this valley also some part of the invading force was in motion—we did not learn what part; but as we were far to one side of their march in this little village, there was no surgeon to help us. Then suddenly came to me a thought of old Dr. Braxton. Where was he? Where were they? And I remembered that in the report made to the officer I had not heard a word about women. Had they been hurt in the *mêlée*, or had they at the first alarm crept away and hidden in some crevice of the mountain, guided by the old darkies, who seemed to know every 'coon-hole in all that region? My head

9

was not very clear then; but I remember that it occurred to me that as the women were not mentioned, and as this cavalry went over the mountain, it was possible that it had not been sent for us especially, and that consequently the Secesh officer Arthur might have had no hand in our fate; but appearances were against him, and nobody else thought as I did about it.

In the course of that day there came a great many darkies about us, women and pickaninnies or very old men; and they were all eager to help us to some little comforts of food and sympathy when not observed by the guards or by the vindictive white women near.   Toward night there was one old man whose odd demeanor attracted my attention; and observing him closely, I saw that he was one who had been with the Braxton family, and who was the Major's principal help as to ways through the mountain.   Immediately my imagination ran wild with the fancy that his appearance here was with some purpose, and that he had a communication to make to some of us.   Presently I made a pretext of wanting to take a few steps down to the end of the barnyard that served for the time as guard-house; so I called this fellow to lend me his shoulder, as my leg had a sabre-cut and I could by this time not bear my weight on that side.   He came as if unwillingly, grumbling and cursing the Yankees; and this I saw was an adroit ruse on the old fellow's part to deceive the guard.   As I bore my elbow on his shoulder and walked slowly with a great deal of pain, he said, in a style that showed his appreciation of time:

"Corp'ral, I seen de Major. He's done gone dead. In his pocket I found dis letter. What shall I do with it?" And he held close to him so I could see just it, a letter he had found in the Major's pocket. It was addressed "To Reuben Pettibone, Esq., Portland, Maine. This letter is to be posted only if found on my dead body;" and below some one had written—perhaps this old Sambo—"done gone knockt on hed wid but eend muskit."

As he hastily thrust this into his coat again, I said to him:

"It ought to go North. Can you send it?"

"Shuah, corp'ral, shuah! Send it by de grapevine telegraph."

That was a postal arrangement much in use then, and equivalent to the "underground railroad" for forbidden travel between the sections.

"Send it, then," I said; "it may be of great importance to his family."

"Send it shuah, boss; wish to golly dis old nigger could do more dan dat."

"Where are the ladies?" I said.

"Guess day'm safe nuff in de mountains, corp'ral." And before I could get more from him he slipped away and was gone; nor was his coming or going much more observed than would have been that of one more fly in a swarm.

But what had really happened in the mountains was as follows:

As soon as the cavalry had swept away, and the

guard detailed had got fairly started down the
mountains with the wounded, this old darky had
been the first to creep out of the hole in which he
had lain hidden through the fight. It was not yet
daylight, but he had fumbled around in the hope that
he could be of some help to those left on the field.
He had found them all, however, beyond his surgery. Then the thought of valuables or papers had
occurred to him ; but the North Carolina fellows
had been ahead of him there, and all he had found
was this letter in the Major's pocket which he had
shown me, and which now, therefore, went forward
with the strange additions to its superscription.

But the Major was not then really dead ; though
the old uncle, who was not an adept in symptoms,
was justified in believing that he was, since he had
received such injuries of the brain as simulated that
condition. No doubt the surgeon of the cavalry
had reported him mortally wounded.

Some hours later the field was looked over by
more instructed eyes than those of the old darky.
Dr. Braxton and the two ladies had, it appears, been
on foot almost as soon as any of us that night at the
first shot ; and foreseeing what might happen, they
had clambered by a narrow zigzag path almost up the
perpendicular wall of the mountain, and looked down
upon the field as if from a swallow's nest in the side
of a cliff, or as if from a cliff-house like those in
the Arizona mountains. As soon as the broadening
light showed that there was no one on foot below,
but only dead or dying men, they all came down.

Miss Phœbe was a brave little spirit, not dismayed by the presence of death. She found the body of the Major, and was the first to discover that there was life in him yet. She watched and was sure she could observe his respiration. Her father soon confirmed her opinion. He found that the Major had a bullet in his brain, and had his skull fractured, perhaps hit with the butt end of a cavalry carabine, but that he was not dead yet.

Thereupon Miss Phœbe declared that she would not leave while he was alive, or that he must be carried to some place of refuge in the mountains where he could be cared for. The old doctor was not a hard-hearted man, as we all knew; but surgeons are apt to suppose that a man who has but a few hours to live can die as well in one place as another; and as the Major's hurts were certainly mortal, he applied that reasoning to this case.

But Phœbe said:

"Father, we are Christians, at least; and this officer, though he thought himself compelled to do toward us acts that were those of an enemy, did all with a high-minded gentlemanly courtesy that it would be barbarous in us to forget when evil has come upon him."

"Yes, brother," said Aunt Hetty; "Phœbe is right about this. We cannot leave him to die like a stricken animal by the wayside."

"And besides," said Phœbe, "if one of our own circle—dear me! it is terrible to say it, but it must be said, and will be said—if Arthur had a hand in this!"

"Arthur!" said the old gentleman, as if such a thought had not dawned upon him. "Impossible, child!"

"He was dreadfully angry when he went away," said Phœbe.

And Aunt Hetty tried to say a word, but broke down in an overwhelming burst of tears.

Thereupon the doctor went away to see some other wounded ones, and left them to their own devices.

CHAPTER XII.

FROM the spot where he was knocked over, the Major was carried by the contrabands whom Phœbe called to help her, to a place called Skibbevan, about a mile or two away by rough mountain footpaths. It was the thoughtfulness of one of the colored assistants that suggested this refuge; for little Phœbe was at her wits' ends on this subject. She knew they were too far from Braxton House to go there with the wounded man, even if Braxton House still had a roof upon it; and where else to go she could not imagine, for she probably did not know at just what point of the mountain they then were.

Then a yellow girl of about Phœbe's age who stood by, and who was in full sympathy with the lady in this gentle service, said softly:

"Might take him to our house, Missus Phœbe."

"What is your house?"

"Skibbevan."

"Yes," said Phœbe, "that is it; take him there. I'm glad you spoke. You are Agate?"

"Yes, miss."

So they went to Agate's home.

Skibbevan was Phœbe's own property. It had

been left her by an aunt who had died in Phœbe's
infancy. But it was not a productive estate; and
when Agate's mother—old Naomi, who had been
Phœbe's nurse—married a miller, the place had
been given them for a home, and they ground corn
and oats for use at Braxton House to pay the rent.
And now for the first time in her life Phœbe rejoiced that she was the owner of this hitherto
nearly worthless old place.

Skibbevan was a stone mill, crumbled with age;
for it had been built many and many a year before,
and in the times when no house was of use in that
region unless it was also a fort. There was a tradition that it was the first home of a civilized man
whose windows ever looked across the Shenandoah
Valley. It stood in a croft scooped in the side of
the mountain, perhaps by the action of the ancient
torrent, the remains of which now placidly turned
the old wheel of the mill; and it was so placed that
the edges of the croft completely hid the house from
the view of those coming down the valley or going
up, and to get a fair view of it from the valley one
had to be well to the other side of that picturesque
expanse and very nearly opposite the mill. Its
builder's name had passed away forever from the
memory of man, but from its own name it was
reasoned that the builder had been some adventurous Englishman of the early colonial times who, in
the Turkish wars or as a prisoner in the hands of
the Saracens, had acquired some Eastern lore, since
Skibbevan was supposed to be a corruption of the

name of one of the four Beautiful Places, or para-
dises, of Oriental story.

Persons who pretended to know, but whose pretended knowledge may have been all imagination,
said that in the days when Greenway Court was a
famous scene of colonial hospitality, many hardy
adventurers who went to and fro between that
forest home and tide-water tried different paths and
went different ways into the wilderness, and, sick-
ened with the experiences and disappointments of
the life of the time, made themselves homes here
as in the bosom of primitive nature, and that Skibbevan was built for one of these.

In recent times there had been added to the old
stone structure, on the other side from the mill-
wheel, a wooden wing, with two capacious rooms
on the ground-floor, and an ample piazza; and thus
it was altogether a roomy and habitable place,
kept in good order by neat old Naomi and her
energetic and industrious husband Hiram.

"De Lord help us! who's dat voice I hear down
dar?" said old Naomi from the kitchen in the tower,
as Phœbe gave some directions to the men and
women when they reached the steps of the piazza.
"Dat my blessed child, shuah."

And in another second the old woman was out
and held Phœbe in her arms, with all the natural
impulse and energy of a warm heart.

"Heard drefful news, drefful news," she said.
"Heard dat sojers carry away old doctor, Aunt

Hetty, my baby, everybody; burn Braxton House, ruin de whole world. And all dis night I pray to de Lord Jesus to help us out of dis, and dere, now, you comes like a voice from heaven to comfort yer old Naomi. But land o' Goshen! what's dis?" she said, as her eye caught in the folds of the shawl the blood-stained face of the Major.

Agate, who saw that Phœbe could not stand much of this, hastily led the old woman away, and the others carried the Major up and laid him gently on the piazza.

"In a jiffy," as the old woman said, Agate had told her all that had taken place, and given her such a glimpse of the circumstances as to show the need of discretion and tranquillity, both for the sake of the wounded man and the already overwrought sensibilities of the lady; and then Naomi and Agate came in together, and soon prepared in front of the large window of the best room a comfortable fresh bed, upon which the Major was laid.

Naomi managed heroically to hold her tongue until this was done, and all she said then was:

"Bless us, chile, how dis will 'stonish Hiram! But Hiram's doin' bosin's work with all de men he could get over to Braxton, tryin' to put out de fiah."

Water was brought, and Phœbe herself, kneeling down beside the bed, washed the pale, handsome face of the Major with her dainty white taper fingers, and disentangled his hair, matted in masses with the clotted blood.

"Massy on us!" said Naomi, as they all thus saw

the Major's face, "dat's a mighty handsome man.
But 'tain't Mas'r Art'ur."

They all wanted to help; but Phœbe seemed
jealous that any but she should touch him, and
herself placed his head upon the pillow and moistened his lips with fresh cool water. For an instant,
however, she felt faint, and nearly fell to the floor
as she came upon the bruised mouth of the wound
where the ball had entered his skull, and from which
the blood still slowly oozed away.

Agate lifted her up and led her out to the piazza,
and said softly:

"He is as comfortable now as you can make him.
Leave him for a little. It's too much for any one."

Naomi rushed away to the kitchen to prepare a
cup of coffee, because she was "sure her dear baby
needed something to strengthen her;" but the poor
old woman was as anxious on this occasion to conceal
the outburst of her own clamorous sorrow as to help
Phœbe. Agate a moment later slipped away to the
kitchen also; and Phœbe, left alone, went into the
room again, kneeled beside the bed, and put up the
prayer of a pure-hearted, gentle, earnest little
maiden.

"God grant that this wound may not be mortal;
that all those whose hearts will be broken to hear
of his death may be spared that blow."

She could not accept as the last word the calm
declaration of surgical science that the bullet which
penetrates a man's brain necessarily destroys life.
She had a hope beyond that, and she put her hopes

in her prayers—a grand help in such difficulties, for under the worst inflictions the person who has not the heart to say a word to any other person about them finds a happy resource in those silent appeals of faith which need not be limited by any conventional views of facts, nor by anybody's opinion of what is or is not possible. It is only in prayer that people can still express the hope that that will happen which judgment declares is impossible.

In half an hour Aunt Hetty arrived also; for she had followed more slowly the steps of Phœbe, because Skibbevan was an immediate and accessible refuge; and some hours later the old doctor came, because where Phœbe and Hetty were was the world to him.

They all stayed there quietly that day. Hetty, Naomi, and Agate watching Phœbe; Phœbe beside the Major; and the old doctor on the piazza pacing to and fro, chafing at his trouble as at a chain, and from time to time stopping in front of the open window to watch from that little distance the Major on his bed, and then with a negative shake of the head, of which perhaps he was scarcely conscious, continuing his to-and-fro march.

It was planned that at night the doctor should go over the mountain to ascertain the real state of Braxton House, to see what could be saved, and to stay there if this might prevent wanton destruction of the property by stragglers and marauders. Meanwhile Hetty and Phœbe were entirely at home at Skibbevan.

Before he departed at night, the doctor went in and examined once more the Major's wounds. He thought the penetrating wound was made by a pistol-ball, and in the close hand-to-hand fight, for the hair was burned as if by the flash of the pistol.

"He has a hard head," said the doctor, "or that ball would have gone completely through and out at the other side. Unless," he continued, "the Confederate cartridges are made with bad powder; and probably they are. Everybody cheats our government and people."

But the doctor satisfied himself that the ball had really pierced the skull and entered the brain. He believed it had ranged upward. It went in somewhere above the left ear, and was lying near the top of the head. But he would not put in an instrument to ascertain this.

"Poor fellow," he said, "he is near enough to his end. I will not poke out with probes the little that is left of his life. For a Northern man he was the most thorough gentleman I ever met."

Perhaps if the doctor's opinion of the Major had been a trifle less favorable, he might have finished him then and there with his probes, as I believe I have seen many a fine fellow finished in a field-hospital.

It was the doctor's opinion, furthermore, that in addition to the wound from the bullet there was a fracture of the skull from a bad blow on the top of the head; but this wound did not now seem to him as bad as he at first thought it.

"Nevertheless," he said, "the bullet-wound is more than enough. He cannot live."

By this time some change had taken place in the condition of the Major. He had at first been cold, and those who had tried to count the beat of his pulse could not find the pulse. This was the condition that made the old Sambo who had first gone to him before day believe he was dead; and this state was produced probably by the overwhelming shock due to the great injuries the brain had received. But later in the day he had rallied a little from this; his pulse had become perceptible and there was some warmth, and he had shown as much life as is implied in the feeling of thirst, for when Phœbe moistened his lips he drew them into his mouth as if to get the fluid that was left upon them.

· "He appeared at first," said the doctor, "as if he would die without recovering from the shock; and they are apt to die that way from these severe lesions of the brain. But there is a reaction, and there will be fever, and maybe delirium and mania, and he will die exhausted from these, or from the pressure of blood as hemorrhage continues within the skull. Reaction, as it comes on, has sometimes an encouraging effect, because it seems to be a recovery of the vital forces. It is only, however, the slower way of dying from such wounds. He cannot recover; not but what men have recovered from dreadful wounds of the brain perhaps as bad as this. Baron Larrey gives such a case. But this will not resemble that. He cannot live short of a miracle."

"But miracles happen," said Phœbe, who caught these last words.

Now, the old doctor did not believe that miracles happen; but he would not disturb Phœbe on that point, so he went out and said no more.

Some of this account of the condition of her patient Phœbe heard; the rest was gently suggested rather than told her; but she stayed by the Major and kept up her hopes just the same, and all that night she and Agate watched by turns at the bedside, and Naomi prayed out in the mill.

CHAPTER XIII.

THE PETTIBONE FAMILY.

SLOWLY and less surely than was common, the letter found upon Pembroke's body went on its way to the North, as the old uncle had said it would, by "grapevine telegraph." Now, the "grapevine telegraph" and the "underground" railroad were organizations of the same general nature; that is to say, as the one carried forbidden passengers by secret and difficult ways, the other transmitted communications surreptitiously if not always swiftly. From hand to hand of trusty negroes it went down the valley and over the Potomac, until it was actually deposited in the post-office at Frederick City in Maryland. But from that point northward its journey was slower, for near Baltimore the whole mail fell into the hands of a troop of rebel raiders, and the pouch which contained this letter was, with others that the enemy were unable to carry away, cast into the Potomac River. Many months later these pouches were fished out of the river, and the mail went once more on its northward way.

As we have seen, the letter was addressed to Reuben Pettibone, Esq., and it will probably interest the reader to know that this Reuben Pettibone was the Major's father-in-law.

Reuben Pettibone had been a very prosperous man in his time, and with that gentle and excellent woman his wife, his daughter Lætitia, and his son Jack, had been regarded by many of his neighbors as the salt of the earth; for they were rich, perhaps a trifle proud, which does not hurt as the world goes, and they seldom neglected the assertion of their superiority to ordinary mortals. Mrs. Pettibone was in these particulars an exception. She was simpler and gentler, a very lovable old lady; while for the others people felt regard, respect, esteem, but seldom used with relation to them words of a warmer quality.

In the heyday of the family fortunes Lætitia had become the wife of Geoffrey Pembroke, for she was a girl who had her way in the family; and while Pembroke was not so rich a man as Pettibone would have liked for his daughter, he was not very poor; and he was the very man for whom twenty other girls were dying, wherefore Lætitia was determined to have him. Pembroke was much envied, for it was a "good match." Papa was very rich, and the girl was certainly handsome, and of an amiable disposition so far as anybody could know without the opportunity that domestic life gives for a more intimate test.

But it proved an ill-assorted marriage, and they were not happy. Lætitia's temper was of a sort that made it very difficult for any one to be happy near her; and the domestic position of a son-in-law does not often assist in such a case. Sons-in-law

10

have a status that varies from that of warm affection to that of a scarcely-disguised common enemy; and while this status may depend in a great many cases upon the man's nature, it is oftener determined by the nature of his wife. Life in the Pettibone family had become nearly impossible to Pembroke; life in a home of his own there was no chance for, since the rich girl brought up in one way would not live in another; and a point of dissolution was near when another trouble came.

Reuben Pettibone, who was not an extremely rich man, had made some unfortunate speculations early in the war, and while he was in difficulty with this struggle there were suddenly developed with his signature some very heavy notes which he said were forgeries. But this declaration the bankers did not accept; they do not commonly accept a theory against their own interest. They were forgeries, however, and Pettibone would not pay.

Then arose the inquiry, If Reuben Pettibone did not make these notes, who did? The bankers alleged that it was some member of his family, and in their secret investigations they even named Jack Pettibone, the son, a wild fellow, a spendthrift and scapegrace. As soon as Reuben and Harriet, his wife, heard this they feared it might be true, and they brooded over it many days, and talked over it many nights; and the pride was taken out of Reuben, and he was like another man.

Between Reuben and Harriet it was judged that to be poor was a less fearful thing than such a stigma; that the disgrace could not be endured even if it came alone; while they saw beyond it the chances of State prison for Jack, who was, however, just now safely out of reach in Europe.

But just as hard-fisted Reuben had been brought to this point the bank detectives came forward and muddled thinks beautifully with a new theory. They had satisfied themselves that it was not the son, but the son-in-law. As soon as this word was whispered to Reuben in profound secrecy, he tightened his jaws, and buttoned up his pocket, and would not pay. "That fellow might go to prison and rot there for all he cared." But Jack's mother, too wise to venture a judicial investigation on that point, held that the decision to pay must be maintained, and the notes were paid; but the glory of the Pettibone family was cut down, and they lived in a different style and in a smaller house.

All could stand this fall easier than Lætitia; and if she had really loved Pembroke the sacrifice might have been easy for her; but as she weighed him in the scale against her pride, she hated him as the cause of this dreadful mortification. And he, poor fellow, went quietly on and never heard a syllable of the implication of his name, for that part alone no one had ventured to tell him. It was as if they all held tenaciously by this last thread of theory that seemed to save the good name of Jack, and were afraid it might be broken.

But this point came out—was "thrown up" to Pembroke in a moment of anger.

Lætitia's life, as now shaped, seemed like penury to her by comparison with what had been, and she reproached herself daily as one who had brought into the family the author of this disaster, and it seemed to her an outrage that Pembroke should take things so calmly and even seem to be happier than before. Wherefore she said to him one day as she found him in a merry humor:

"You ought to be ashamed to laugh in this house, where your crime has made so many people miserable."

He looked at her for a moment in mute amazement, and then said:

"Oh! do they say I had something to do with it?"

"They know that you did it," she said, and in a few indignant sentences she laid before him the latest form of the detective theory.

He made no answer to all this, but went out on the piazza, lit a cigar, and paced to and fro there for an hour.

He was a thoughtful, calm, wise fellow. An intuition, a sympathy between himself and the only other affectionate soul in that house, Jack's poor old mother, helped him to understand the case; and the image of that poor mother as she might be if awakened from this delusion of the detectives swam in his mind.

He did not go into the house again, but when all was quiet he buttoned up his coat, walked across the fields to town, caught a night train to Boston, went thence to New York, enlisted in a regiment then there on its way to the war, and about ten days later was up to his knees in the Virginia mud.

Jack's mother was the only one upon whom this departure had much effect; for Geoffrey also called her mother, and was always a pleasant presence to her, and she was uneasy and fidgety until they heard where Pembroke was from some one who saw him in the army.

For months together, then, the desolate mother sat in the little window-space, wordless but busy; and the steel rods came and went, came and went, all that winter as she knitted socks for soldiers. They kept up no communication with Geoffrey; but some day some of these socks might make his feet the warmer; or if some other mother's knitting warmed his feet, hers might warm the feet of that other mother's boy.

And Jack!—who could tell? They never heard of him any more; but like a boy who loved his country he might have come home and enlisted too, and might be in the swamps of Virginia, loading and firing for the Union like the rest of them; and she might be so happy as to clothe those dear feet, even.

And so the white thin fingers worked on forever in the little sunshiny window, and the kitten in the sunny place on the floor played with the ball of yarn, till there came a day when Harriet did not feel strong enough to get up from her bed.

They sat with her a few days and a few nights. On the fourth day, just about dawn, Reuben, who was then alone with her, heard her calm, clear voice

call his name, and went to the bedside. Her face
was white with a bluish ashy whiteness, and the
features sharper than before. She said to him:

"Dear Reuben, be very gentle always to Geoffrey;
and if it should be Jack after all"—a hiccough stopped her voice for a moment, and then she went on
again—"if it should be Jack, never forget the great
generosity of Geoffrey's silence."

And that was the last the gentle, loyal mother
ever said. Alas! no one had stood between her and
the blow. She had understood that Jack was the
culprit, though the very fiction of another's guilt had
eased it for her a little. But her words were a rev-
elation to Reuben and never went out of his mind;
for to him Geoffrey's departure had been a "flight,"
and a flight meant guilt.

But while the gentle mother's thoughts had in all
the time before her death been upon the comfort of
the far-away ones, Lætitia had been much occupied
in an altogether different way. She had had good
legal advice to the effect that the departure of Pembroke was an abandonment, and that abandonment
was a good cause for divorce. She had regularly
sought a divorce, therefore, and despite the inevitable delays of the law her application made hopeful
progress until it was known that Pembroke was in
the army. Then the case went on more slowly, and
was not completed when that missive arrived which
we have heard of in Virginia.

Pembroke's letter to Pettibone was in these
words:

"In a stray copy of a Portland paper I saw the notice of mother's death; and if she ever believed that the notes were forged by me, I hope she believed it to the last. Between her and a dreadful blow I was always willing to stand at any cost to myself.

"But neither you nor Lætitia are persons with heart enough to be much hurt on that side; and a wound coming through your pride is what I would wish you may have. Be assured, therefore, by this declaration, if you were not before, that those forgeries were never done by me. It has been always my intention to tell you this face to face when the right time should come; but a soldier is not sure of his life from hour to hour, and I take precaution that you may surely know it. This letter is written to be carried upon my person—marked with directions that if at any time I shall be found dead upon a field of battle, this letter will be posted by the person who buries me.

"You can receive it only in those circumstances. At the same time, therefore, that it takes from your pride the consolation that I do not mean you shall have at my cost, it will give you the good news that I am no more.

"Yours as you may take me,
"GEOFFREY PEMBROKE."

In the tranquil tone of this rather blunt missive—that was cynical, yet did not parade its cynicism; that called the dead one mother, yet had no hysterical

tenderness in it; that was as sincere and downright
as Pettibone had known him who wrote it from his
boyhood up—the father saw the full dawn of a truth
that had already glimmered at the horizon of his
thoughts.

"And he is dead too," said Reuben; "and she is
dead, and Jack is gone. Only two left of us. Well,
well! How pleasant it must be to lie down and
forget all!"

Reuben gave one indication that this communication did not run in the commonplace groove of
life. He did not mention it to Lætitia. She nevertheless soon knew all about it, for the singular superscription had attracted attention in the post-office,
and had been a great deal talked about, and many
easy inferences were made; so that the report spread
that the Pettibones had news from the army that
Pembroke was dead, and Lætitia was asked about it.

Thereupon Lætitia rushed home, ransacked her
father's tables and desks, found the letter and read
it with sarcastic comment upon its reference to herself, and with exulting satisfaction at the close.

"Well," she said, "that changes things. I'm glad
I kept the mourning I wore for ma. Crape feels
horrid against the skin, but they make it in pretty
shapes now. Hum! hum! What shall I wear?
This saves what the divorce-suit would have
cost."

And she sat down and reflected upon the advantageous position in society of the widow of a gallant
fellow who had died for his country.

As a widow of that variety she would enjoy social advantages of which she had been deprived. But a few days before she had been a person occupying a somewhat equivocal position—a married woman without a husband; abandoned, yet not free; and her opinion of her absent lord was such as women of a vixen-like nature commonly hold toward all persons who have in any way caused them the chagrin of mortified vanity.

People would now say that that quiet fellow Pembroke had not been the sort of man to strut up and down the street of the town in a blue coat and brass buttons and exult in the empty glorifications of war, but had gone away without a word and enlisted as a private soldier in a regiment which had proved one of excellent fighting qualities, and that in such company he had won his epaulets. He would therefore be suddenly a famous fellow in the speeches of all men and women, and Lætitia as his bereaved widow would enjoy this *post-mortem* glory.

There was a great deal of patriotic spirit in that neighborhood, and such an association as Lætitia now had with the fame of a dead soldier was the best possible title to social consideration. It gave precedence over claims of family and even wealth; and thus it would happen that many ladies who since the fall in the Pettibone fortunes had scarcely been able to see Lætitia when they met her would now always see her, and rush at her with the warmth of fashionable adulation. She would consequently have the opportunity to settle some old scores by turning the cold shoulder now.

"And I will do it, too," she said. "But shall I wear a crape bonnet or one of those new-fashioned hats?"

CHAPTER XIV.

THERE was one person in Maine who was not altogether pleased with the turn that things had thus taken. This was Mr. Chipperton Chawpney—or Lawyer Chawpenny, as the people called him. This gentleman argued that his true name was Chorpenning, shortened accidentally by careless pronunciation; but the people insisted that it was Chawpenny. He wrote it Chawpney, and thus compromised between prejudice and theory. He was one of the rising men of that region; a bright lawyer, who had gained some important cases, had been in the legislature, and seemed to see his way clear to a fine practice at a future period. He had been Lætitia's counsel in the divorce proceedings, and was an ardent admirer of the lady.

As an admirer it might be supposed he would rejoice that she was now so easily free of the antecedent matrimonial restraint, even though as a lawyer he had to regret the loss of a good bit of important practice. But it was not so. He had indeed hoped that Lætitia would be under obligation to his devotion as an advocate for her freedom, and that gratitude would open the way to her heart; and whereas in that position he was the only aspirant for the hand that he saw would be an object of pursuit, now that she was plainly, obviously, ostentatiously free he had a score of rivals, and almost despaired of his prospects in that direction.

Inspired by the difficulties that thus presented themselves, Chawpney went into the paradise in which Lætitia was now happy, and whispered dreadful things. He said to somebody, one day, that nobody knew of the death of Pembroke except from his own account, and that he himself, as counsel for several life-insurance companies, was always inclined to doubt a man's report of his own death. As to the notion that some wounded soldiers had confirmed the report, who had seen any of these soldiers?

This was reported; and when it fell upon the ears of those women, wives and daughters of quartermasters and sutlers, to whom as the widow of a hero Lætitia now turned the cold shoulder of superiority, it found a fertile soil and grew luxuriantly.

In a little while everybody except Lætitia seemed to know the precise detail of the circumstances by which "that fellow Pembroke" had fooled his innocent and too credulous wife with a story of his death. Some could even tell how he had gone over to the enemy with a part of his company and invented a story to cover the dreadful shame. Again there was a fall in the pride of the Pettibone family, and the heart-broken Lætitia, when she heard of all this, confessed to herself that

even in death—if there was any death about it—
her husband was "a scalawag."

Chawpney did not call upon Mrs. Pembroke to
offer condolences in her bereavement. Indeed, he
only knew her professionally, and did not venture
upon such a liberty. Mrs. Pembroke, however,
called upon him at his office in regard to the proceedings for divorce undertaken by him in her interest. She wished to know the present position
of that suit.

"Well, Mrs. Pembroke," he said, opening very
widely his twinkling light-colored little eyes, "you'll
excuse my saying so, but you astonish me a great
deal by this inquiry."

"Astonish you?" she said. "How so?"

"Why, really, really, Mrs. Pembroke— Ah! I see
how it is; in your trouble, in the confusion of mind
that has followed upon this sad incident, you have
forgotten."

"Forgotten what?" she said, rather shortly.

"Well, it appears by my books," he said, leisurely
turning over some written leaves as he spoke, "I
received instructions from you, or professedly from
you, to discontinue entirely the proceedings for divorce of Lætitia Pembroke against Geoffrey Pembroke."

"Is it possible?" she said. "Instructions from
me?"

"Well, unless this has been done in your name,
but without authority, by some other person."

"No, no," she said, "I do remember; I did it

myself. It happened in this way. At that time
we had just received a report from the army that
Mr. Pembroke had been killed in a battle; and as
that would naturally make such a suit unnecessary,
and as in a case of death we desire to put aside and
forget all that is disagreeable with regard to the lost
ones, I wrote that in an impulsive moment."

"Yes," he said, "it was quite like your excellent
nature and correct taste to desire to forget the evil
that others had done you; but in this case a little, as
you say, impulsive."

"Yes," she said, "impulsive."

"Yes," he said, "impulsive."

And then she waited and hoped he would go on;
but he didn't. He could perceive when a lady had
come upon a pumping expedition as readily as any
man in Maine.

"Since that," she said, "we have heard some reports that incline us to believe that there may be
some deception."

"Ah!"

"Yes; we have heard a story that Mr. Pembroke
is not really dead."

Chawpney only answered with his eyebrows,
which he lifted nearly to the roots of his hair—
whitish, short, wide-awake-looking hair.

"Perhaps," she said, "you have yourself some
knowledge upon this subject."

"Well," he said, "I have heard what is perhaps
the same report that you refer to. In fact, it has
been printed and discussed in all the newspapers,

and everybody has heard it.   It is a public scandal.
But I have no knowledge apart from that."

"Perhaps you have heard of somewhat similar
cases."

"Madam," and little Chawpney assumed an air
of impressive energy as he said this, "the detective
police has a ponderous record of the names of men
who married in the North and, forming perhaps new
connections elsewhere, have procured the publication
of the report of their death in battle, and who,
wronging our real heroes by this seizure of a fame
they do not deserve, are rejoicing in their villany
with the facile Delilahs of Southern lands.   But
pardon my warmth; I forgot for the moment that
your husband—"

"Not at all," said Mrs. Pembroke.   "My husband
may very likely be one of these; and I wish, if the
proceedings can be renewed—"

"Oh, certainly; there has been no court since,
and the discontinuance is on my books merely."

"Then I wish the proceedings to go on," she said;
and the bereaved widow, at Chawpney's suggestion,
gave him full authority to act for her, first as to
the important point of getting evidence whether
Pembroke were dead or alive, and next to obtain
the divorce if he were alive; but to push the proceedings with the greatest possible energy if he
found there was any truth in these stories of mis-
conduct and going over to the enemy, because she,
as a patriotic woman, "could not for a moment en-

dure the thought of continuing relations with a man who was a traitor to his country."

Chawpney mentioned that afternoon to several persons in the town that "Mrs. Pembroke was a noble woman and an honor to her sex, and had spoken words in his office that day which the ancient Spartans would have written in letters of gold upon the pediment of the temple." And the same night he left for New York City to prosecute his inquiries into the fate of "that fellow her husband."

· There was at that time a daily paper called *The News*, which was a convenient and recognized medium of communication between the several sections of the country. People in the South who wanted to communicate family news to their friends resident in the North, or to their friends who, taken prisoners by the army, were detained in the North, got advertisements into that paper in some way; and people in the North who wanted to communicate with the South put their communications into that sheet as personal advertisements, with the certainty that the newspaper would get through the lines, though their letters would not.

Every time a copy of that sheet got through the lines the Southern papers reproduced all these notices; and all Southern soldiers in Northern prisons eagerly secured it in the hope to hear from home.

Chawpney resorted to this medium. He might have found some wounded soldiers of the Major's regiment if he had sought diligently, but he did not want the most direct information. Intelligence colored in the medium of an enemy's mind might be more to his purpose. He inserted an advertisement calling for information of the present whereabouts and condition of Geoffrey Pembroke, late a major of volunteers in the Union army, and "now or recently in hiding somewhere in the Shenandoah Valley." He received from a rebel soldier detained as a prisoner of war at David's Island, in the East River, a response which induced him to visit that soldier. David's Island was a place in which several hundred prisoners were kept, but not in the way in which our fellows were kept at Andersonville and Libby.

David's Island was, in fact, one of Uncle Sam's national watering-places. There were the salty air, the stiff sea-breeze fresh from the Sound, and the green water of the seaside; and there also the pleasant rambles under trees such as we find in a summer resort in the hilly country. Roomy, clean, brightly whitewashed dormitories filled long pavilions recently constructed; and tempting long tables at meal-time reminded one of summer hotels, only there was more to eat than the average summer hotel vouchsafes. Not one in ten of the Southern soldiers, the "white trash" of the Southern States, was ever half so well housed or fed at home as in that prison; and here, coming broken down from Southern battle-fields, they fed up and recovered their *morale*. Rampant rebels resident in the North visited and encouraged them, and they discussed constitutional theories.

11

Nothing there astonished Chawpney so much as his observation of the little industries they fell into to earn money for tobacco. Uncle Sam did not supply tobacco.

"Why," said Chawpney, "these chivalrous gentlemen from the Southern States can actually whittle a stick, and that as handily as any Yankee that ever flourished a jack-knife. From one piece of wood they will cut an imitation of a whole open fan. Nutmegs are nothing to it."

Now, the soldier from whom Chawpney had heard was, like so many others. there, a North Carolina man, and belonged to that regiment which had gone over Company H in the night at Corkscrew Cut. He was one of those who had been wounded in that collision, and was so badly wounded that he had lain for a good while between life and death in one of the houses in that village to which we were all taken after the fight. Just as he had nearly recovered he had been captured by a movement of our cavalry. He consequently knew the news of the neighborhood—or thought he knew it—for a period of several months subsequently to the time when the Major had been left for dead on the field. But as the Braxtons were, in taking any care of the Major, really giving aid and comfort to a wounded enemy, it is to be supposed that they would keep secret about it; wherefore this soldier's news could only be a series of the accumulated guesses of the people down in the valley. But, guesses or real news, this soldier said that the Major's wounds had not proved so bad as were at first reported, and that he had got entirely well; and that if he had not returned he was a deserter, because that country was now all inside the Nothern lines.

Meantime there had been at home in Maine some reaction of opinion in the Major's favor; and when Chawpney's report was triumphantly made public it was received with indignation, and some friends of the Major demanded that an inquiry so important should not stop at so unsatisfactory a point. There was a movement started, indeed, to send some one down to hunt the Major up, on the theory that if alive he must be helpless somewhere and ought to be rescued; with the alternative notion that if he was a deserter indeed, the name of an honorable family was involved, and that family should be the first to give up its recreant scion.

Chawpney heard of this proposition with dismay, but was equal to the occasion. He represented to Lætitia that she should herself go on this expedition to show her duty as a good wife, and volunteered to accompany her. He represented that Frederick in Maryland, Winchester in Virginia, Leesburg, and other places were all comfortable towns in which she could be as secure as at home, and from these points or some one of them efficient inquiries could be made.

Lætitia saw in this scheme of an expedition some attractive features, and they went.

They first went to Washington, taking some letters of introduction to friends there; and as it was

now rainy weather, and the roads were taking on a
wintry condition, they were much advised against
the attempt to pursue their efforts in Virginia just
then.   Washington was gay also, and Lætitia enjoyed its social pleasures, while Chawpney improved the occasion to work up some political
schemes. They halted for a time at a pleasant
stage, and cultivated a knowledge of one another.
Lætitia had by this time become fully aware of
Chawpney's ambition with respect to herself.

CHAPTER XV.

MAJOR PEMBROKE did not die.

Upon Dr. Braxton's return from the journey made to save some of his property, he was astonished to learn that the Yankee major was still alive. He had at first been so certain the Major would die that he had hastened his own return, because of the reflection that the women would be troubled with the difficulties of a funeral; and perhaps, in a true scientific spirit, he had some curiosity to know the precise course that ball had taken in the brain. In the many miseries and disappointments of those days, an interesting autopsy might have been even a distraction and a consolation.

"He is a man of great vitality," said the doctor. "His surviving such a wound for so many days is unusual. It will soon be over, however."

But when four days more had passed and the Major was certainly not losing ground, the doctor began to go oftener to gaze upon him at the open window,—began to arch his eyebrows, and gently scratch the top of his head with the tip end of the middle finger of his right hand.

"Perhaps we may help nature a little and pull him through," he said. "It would be a remarkable recovery. There has been but little apparent hemorrhage; and there cannot have been much concealed within the skull, to judge from his condition. From the direction of that wound—let me see, now!—yes, it has touched the brain in front of the middle meningeal artery; it has passed perhaps diagonally under or inside that artery. If I dared put in a probe now! But no; as I would not put it in at first because there was no hope, it would be murder to put one in now that there may be hope. Perhaps this will prove one of those marvellous lucky cases."

Thus the old man constantly ran on in his surgical lingo, partly talking to himself, partly to those about him, as from hour to hour and from day to day new features of the Major's case presented themselves to his acute perceptions. He was rather an unusual kind of a surgeon, was this old Braxton; for he had comparatively small faith in surgery, but the greatest possible faith in the recuperative forces of nature, just a little helped by surgery over the rough places.

"At Montpellier, in France," he said,—for the doctor was a surgeon who came down from the days when it was believed that no surgical education was complete unless it was rounded up in the hospitals of France,—"at Montpellier, in the museum of the medical school there, I saw a skull with a bullet held against the inner wall by spiculæ of bone which had grown around it. That was the skull of a veteran of the wars of old Napoleon, and the veteran had carried that bullet for forty years. If one soldier, why not another? Then there was the crowbar case. A fellow in the North, somewhere, had a tamping-iron driven through his brain in careless blasting, and he got well. But we must keep the suppuration free. There is the case mentioned by Carnochan, for instance. That fellow died because the wound healed superficially and the suppuration was pent in."

Sometimes the Major was an out-and-out madman in his violence, and but that there was some paralysis of the muscles, he might have done harm. Then his delirium would soften, and he would seem to be recounting various histories; but they never could make out in what he said one distinct word. He seemed to sleep sometimes tranquilly, but would start from it always as from a nightmare.

All the doctor did was to bleed him, and put little hard rolls of lint into the edge of the wound.

There were in the Major's case stages of varying condition; an alternation of mania-like excitement and half-dead tranquillity. Braxton thought that this tranquillity was a consequence of oppression through pent-up fluids that should come away but could not, since a spontaneous appearance of these always made a change.

As one of the periods of great excitement, with heat of the head, came on, while Phœbe slept in the next room, and Agate and Naomi were with the Major, old Naomi, seizing a large, sharp pair of scissors, cut all the hair off the Major's head, quite close to the scalp, in order that she might apply cloths wet with cool water with more facility.

Agate was indignant at this act, and said to her mother :

"De Lord didn't give you no right to cut dat gentleman's hair dat way."

But old Naomi put her aside with a brusque

"Don't bodder me, chile. I nussed folks wid brain-fever 'fore you was thought about."

Phœbe was astonished when she came in ; but she saw the advantage of this, and as she passed her hand, wet with cologne and water, over the Major's head, she made a discovery. At a point on the unwounded side of the cranium she came upon a slight protuberance, a small, round elevation of the surface, of which she spoke to her father.

That was a day of great excitement for the old doctor. He ran his palpigerous fingers two or three times delicately over that nodule, and then straightened himself up and passed both his hands with his fingers open like rakes through his short gray hair as if, feeling a need for more room in his head, he would like to lift the roof off it. Then he walked about the room two or three times without any object, but pretending one object or another ; making believe to shut the door against the draught, though there was no draught, or to open the window, though it was open already ; from all which conduct Phœbe perceived that her papa was " nervous."

Then the old gentleman calmed down somewhat, and settled himself at the bedside with his fingers fastened as if by new nervous attachment on that nodule, and with the unmistakable face of a man who reasons on what he believes he feels, but can see only with the more or less clairvoyant vision of the mind's eye.

At last he said:

"That must be it; the ball is there! But if it is, it has been there all the time; and how did I miss it at first? That is what I cannot make out. But what then? Patients must not be the worse because of a surgeon's adherence to theories that may be founded on error. It ought to come out. And yet, since he has done so well with it there, would not any operation now be an interference with a healing process? Well, well! as it has been so comfortable there all these days, there is no need to be precipitate."

And the doctor went out and tramped the woodland paths on the mountain-side to clear his clogged thoughts.

No doubt it happens often to a good doctor to stand at the turning-point where Braxton then found himself.

He may touch a trouble happily if he acts and so save a life; yet he may also blunder clumsily into some delicate proceeding of curative nature and break it all up. This, if he acts; and if he does not act, the golden moment may go by at which a touch of his art would have given victory in the fight for life.

Some vigorous exercise on the mountain-side

brought the doctor once more to clear and unperturbed perceptions.

It is one of the mysteries of life that an energetic use of the muscles clears the mind with many persons. Cardinal Richelieu and Napoleon are named as persons to whom at times an almost desperate physical activity was necessary. Somehow that activity restores a lost equilibrium. It is as if a stream of vital energy came upon the delicate cerebral machinery and overwhelmed the intellectual operations by its volume and its force; but this stream being turned to drive the mill-wheel of the muscles, the mind gets no more than it wants and goes on smoothly.

As soon as the doctor came in, he quietly told Agate to get him her father's shaving-brush, soap, and razor, which she as quietly did; and the doctor without a word more sat down beside the bed, turned the Major's head easily on the pillow, and lathered and shaved all the space about that little nodule, making it as clean as was possible for one not much used to shaving others.

Then at a sign Phœbe brought a case of instruments from the top of Naomi's bureau, and kneeled beside the bed and hid her face.

Next, as easily as you lay open a roasted chestnut with your pen-knife, Braxton, with two straight cuts that crossed each other at right angles, went to the bone over that nodule, and carefully laid back the four little flaps thus made. He discovered then that a trephine, the absence of which had troubled him, would not have been necessary if he had had it, for the ball had reached this part of the cranium with just enough force left to get clearly through the inner table of the skull, and to crush but not pierce the outer table ; and the comminuted fragments of bone were easily picked away with a forceps.   In fifteen minutes from the time the doctor came in he had the bullet in his hand.

In consequence of this operation the wound drained itself; for the Major's head was pierced through and through, as the ball had hit him on the left side rather higher than the top of the ear, but more to the front, and was taken out at about the same distance above and behind the ear on the other side.

Many times that night the doctor went in and felt his patient's pulse ; and that night it was for the first time satisfactory.   There was gone from it a hard point of irritation that it had never been without. Now it was soft and even ; and at daylight next day Braxton said for the first time confidently that he believed the Major would get well.

But a shade of doubt had already come over the thoughts of some, in that little home, as to the condition he would be in intellectually if he did indeed recover otherwise. Naomi, who was perhaps not more acute than the others, but was certainly more outspoken, had already several times in her blunt words given form to a vague fear.

"Sure's yer born," she said, "I b'lieve dat gentleman loss his sense ; don't know what's goin' on ;

can jes' hear and see; can't hardly say a word; don't want to look at nothin' but Phœbe."

How they first comprehended the Major's condition it is hard to say. There seems to be some knowledge that people acquire more by absorption than perception, and they are themselves unable to give an account of how they came by it. Somebody had at first thought that the Major did not hear, because what was said did not seem to make an impression on his mind, though there was no mania and he was evidently more or less conscious. But having their attention turned to this point of possible deafness and watching acutely, they became satisfied that noises did attract his attention.

He could hear, then; but words spoken to him seemed to awaken no intellectual response. He would indicate by looks of unmistakable satisfaction how agreeable it was to have his pillows changed, or to be helped into a new position when weary with one maintained for many hours; and yet if asked the minute before whether he would like this to be done, he would only turn his large mild eyes toward the questioner with an aspect of uninterested inquiry or weary indifference.

As to all this the doctor expressed no opinion until about ten days after the bullet was out, and that was nearly three weeks from the time the Major was hurt. By that period the Major had made a marvellous progress toward recovery, yet he had never spoken a word, nor seemed to understand one. Then the old doctor said:

"There is no doubt that the third convolution has been in part involved and perhaps disorganized; but there must also have been yet more extensive interference with the functions of the hemispheres."

This did not convey much information to the others until Aunt Hetty, by persistent questioning as to the words "convolutions," "hemispheres," etc., drew out the plain English of what the doctor intended to say; which was that that part of the brain which was most hurt by the bullet was precisely the part which is the seat of the function of speech, and that the Major had probably lost entirely all those intellectual conceptions that lie at the root of the communication of our thoughts or impressions by language. And the doctor also thought that the Major had lost in some greater or less degree the function of memory.

Aunt Hetty was not a woman to be satisfied with any half-knowledge on so new a world of facts as this opened to view, and extorted little by little such information as she could, until she comprehended that the loss of memory might have gone so far as to have blotted out from the man's mind every fact of his life recorded there; and that if the loss of speech was absolute as seemed, it might remain so for what was left of life; or the Major might acquire speech again, word by word, as a child does; or suddenly some day, under the influence perhaps of a great emotion, language, memory, all would come to him again, like a blaze of light.

The doctor made a picturesque comparison to enable Aunt Hetty to distinctly understand this.

"His brain," he said, "his old brain—the brain
he had that night—has been overwhelmed by the
fire and heat and changes of a fierce inflammation,
as some of the ancient cities were overwhelmed and
lost in floods of lava; and a new brain, like a new
city, may grow above it. But some day there may
be a great row in the new city; an accident may
crush a place through the crust, and the streets of
the new and the old will run together."

Meantime the Major, once in a fair way of improvement, went on rapidly, and began really to get
well; and all the little company there, misled at
first as to his sanity by his incapacity to make it
evident, but understanding now how this was, saw
easily enough, hour by hour, that his mind was as
clear as any one's except as to the fact that he was
without speech—or without words, rather, for he
had utterance and talked gibberish.

His possession of the power of speech, that is, so
far as the voice goes merely, was made evident in
a way that at first had a somewhat comical effect.
He seemed to watch intently the lips of persons who
talked, and then to endeavor by mere imitation to
repeat what the person said. He succeeded first
with Naomi. She had not the liberal vocabulary of
the others, perhaps, and therefore depended more
upon a few set phrases which answered for many
occasions. One of these, her customary utterance
of impatience, was, "Don' bodder me, tell yer."

Pembroke caught this up and repeated it like a poll-parrot, and it became with him a name for Naomi. As soon as she came into the room he always said it, to her extreme delight; the more, perhaps, because he repeated so accurately the darky intonation.

He caught a phrase from Agate also, which seemed to answer with him in the same way as a sound of personal identification. This was, "Some o' de essence."   Agate often brought him a bowl of soup, which, as it was made in the kitchen from meat-juice, was a kind of gravy-soup, and all such juices the darkies called essence; and when she brought in this refreshment, never getting well used to his want of comprehension, she always asked, as she would have done with any other, if he would have "some o' de essence."

He associated the sounds with the two as a child calls a dog a "bow-wow."

In the same way he called the old doctor "How is he now?" because that was his customary inquiry; and he called Aunt Hetty "Heigh-ho! says Rowley," for that old dame, sitting for hours quiet with her thoughts, had a habit of coming out with a "Heigh-ho!" and, reflecting that that expression of the sense of the tediousness of things was not complimentary to those about her, had equally acquired the habit of giving her melancholy exclamation a humorous turn by associating it with the old nursery-rhyme.

Pembroke often brought these phrases out in ways so amusingly inappropriate, or even apt, as to make every one very merry, and their laughing seemed to please and cheer him.

But although the Major had no words, it is wonderful how he became the autocrat of that establishment and governed it with his eyes. But this is the common attribute of an invalid around whose bed or chair a little world like that revolves, and toward whom are turned all the sympathies, wishes, and daily and hourly thoughts of a circle of amiable and generous persons.

"But he has a memory, then," said Aunt Hetty one day suddenly, as they fell into a moment of silence after laughing at one of these odd happenings of the Major's names for those about him.

"Yes," said Phœbe; "but papa did not say that his memory was gone in that sense. His memory may be perfect for things to be learned now, but is gone as to what happened before."

"It is like a slate, I suppose," said Hetty, "from which the sums have been wiped off, but upon which new sums may be written."

"Or like a tree stripped in a storm upon which new leaves will grow," said Phœbe.

"How I should like to know whether he was a married man!" said Aunt Hetty; and then no other observation was made for that occasion.

CHAPTER XVI.

PHŒBE SEEKS COUNSEL.

PHŒBE had passed through singular phases of experience in these consecutive months of psychical agitation. For one, she had never believed that the Major's reason was gone. That painful guess was not hers. In the Major's eyes—large, soft, eloquent, rational eyes, that roamed uneasily about the room from point to point when they did not find Phœbe, and rested upon her with supreme tranquillity when she came into view—she saw unmistakably, as she believed, that this man's intellect was a force which had not yet dashed out beyond the control of ordinary human influences.

But the little lady kept this opinion secret.

Next, however, as she heard of a lost memory, merely, and lost speech, and as these losses seemed to indicate only that the accumulations of the intellect were gone, and not the intellect itself,—as it might be the loss of a treasure, but not of the treasure-finder,—the explanation ran concurrently with her own observations, and she accepted it; and the thoughts it suggested opened to her singular speculations upon the future.

Where was all this to end?

12

Before this time every one of all that little company had, as if by a common truce of sympathy, forgotten alike the thought of the morrow, and lived in the daily and even hourly interest they felt for the Major. Picked up at first as a man slain almost in their presence, they had watched over him only to do for him the best services that can be done for any one; and Phœbe, never for a moment imagining that his death was not momentarily imminent, had passed hours on her knees at the bedside with her little morocco-bound prayer-book before her eyes, commending the passing life to the Giver.

But as the fatal stroke was delayed, and death seemed to play with hope, Phœbe earnestly prayed that the brighter possibility might be realized: yet always without any other thought than that of a merciful little Christian who instinctively wishes that the best may come to all.

And thus insensibly from point to point of experience she had grown—without any perception on her own part, entirely without consciousness of it—into such relations of deep sympathy and interest with this man, into such a daily hanging upon his fate,—the fate of an enemy, an accidental person in her life,—that now, when it was recognized he would live, she was startled and amazed as she asked herself, What then?

Some women are themselves equal to every emergency of life; but those hard-headed ones are hard-hearted also. They are gorgons. They are equal to all occasions, simply because no event reaches any sensitive point in their natures.

All the lovable little women, however, instinctively want help, and differ from one another only as to the points in the compass of life toward which they turn to look for it. But this is a result that is determined by the character of the woman. Some have friends—men or women, as the case may be—whose advice pierces all the clouds of doubt. Some have a brother; some go to mother, some to father; and some hie quietly away to a dim corner of the church and pray for divine assistance.

Phœbe, if she had had a mother, would have gone to her with all the vague thoughts which she could not herself formulate, but which concerned the new possibilities of the Major's recovery. She had no mother; and though Aunt Hetty was there, she did not go to her, because that goodly dame's advice would, she knew, be framed entirely on those aspects of the case which were perceptible to the intellect; while the cry of an impulsive heart and a warm, emotional nature would not, she believed, be heard in that court.

Phœbe's only resource was a dim corner in a little out-of-the-way church, to be reached by the beautiful woodland paths, to which she went every night, with Agate for company.

In those days religion was kept alive, like the sacred fire upon the Caucasian hill, by inner impulses, and with little assistance from church ceremonial. Nevertheless the church was there; a dim, silect, mystic corner of this stormy earth, like the hither end of a solemn vista whose other end is be-yond the stars; and there, sometimes, there was even service, for a tough-minded soldier-preacher from Winchester now and then made godly raids through the wilderness to comfort the faithful.

Phœbe was not a devotee. But they are in error who suppose that the only form which piety assumes in woman is an absolute negation of all of life but what is related to the formalities and seasons of religious services. She was not a very religious person. She was not a wicked woman, certainly; far from it, indeed. Neither was she an oppressively goody-goody one. She was in this respect about as the world of agreeable women are. They are not the devil's daughters, because they have been brought up, as the phrase goes, to fear the Lord,— and do indeed fear those things that are threatened in all religious schemes. Neither are they quite given up to the law and the gospel, because a bright-witted little lady does not surrender the im-pulses of a feminine nature to a rule that would suppress even an extra blue ribbon on a summer's day.

It was warm human blood that was in Phœbe's veins, and not holy-water; and yet those trips to the church were a comfort to her, if for no other reason than that they satisfied her mind that she was taking the best advice upon her difficulties.

From that time Phœbe's thoughts and her whole life ran strictly and simply in the way of nature.

Destiny had thrown her and the Major together in this singular way; and watching over him day by day, she, with all the rest indeed, had grown to feel a tender regard for him. And then as his recovery had gone on and made famous progress, it had fallen especially to her lot to sit with him through the winter days in Naomi's room, and through the long days of the next summer on that piazza; and she had indeed retaught him, so far as he knew it, his mother-tongue. From that dainty mouth he had caught and learned once more the wonderful trickeries of speech.

That they should fall irretrievably in love with one another was not merely inevitable. It would have been a treason against the divine law which made woman for man and man for woman, if it had happened otherwise.

For the world, even, admits all the authority of that divine rule, with this limitation only: that there shall be no existing contrary obligation. And where was there any contrary obligation in this case?

Arthur on one side, you will say, and the people in Maine upon the other. Nobody had ever heard a word of Arthur since the time he left the camp that night about ten months before; and when a man has not made even the littlest ripple upon the surface of the sea of life in that time, and when such silence in a soldier coincides with a period in which there has been a battle, with ten thousand killed and wounded on either side, and when hundreds of those left on "fame's eternal camping-ground" were recorded as unknown, everybody assumes that he was probably one of the unrecognized dead.

As the Major's past life was erased from his own brain, he also seemed to be as completely erased from the record that life elsewhere had kept of him. They could not doubt that he had been reported as killed that night, and that his friends, wherever and whoever they were, had accepted that report as the end of the story. Therefore, as he was lost to his friends and they lost to him, what was there in all his actual life but what had occurred in this valley? They were like two shipwrecked and cast alone on some beautiful island in a summer sea—lost to the world, as the world to them; yet all the world to one another.

Therefore Phœbe knew well that love for her was the one impulse of Pembroke's life months before there could be any words exchanged upon that subject; and he knew—it was the first delicious discovery of a new life—that, heart and soul, Phœbe was his.

Neither was there any one near to be surprised as all this made itself plain, for all had seen it grow. With Aunt Hetty, with Naomi, with Agate, it had become a matter of course. And when they went to the little church one day in the beautiful sunset-hour and were married, if any there thought it perilous for Phœbe's future, they thought also that it was an inevitable stroke of destiny.

But it might not have gone to this if Dr. Braxton

had remained on the scene. He had indeed been often made uneasy by the thought of Phœbe's relation to the Major, and had repeatedly said to Hetty, "We do not know this man's history; who he is or what he is. He certainly may have a wife at his home in the North." Braxton had even caused some inquiry to be made by his friends for a Pembroke family in New York, but had found none; a fact due, of course, to the circumstance that the Major, though in a New York regiment, was from another State.

Her father's objection to the marriage, if he had been there to make it, would have been the last word of the law to Phœbe; but he was not there. He passed in these days the greater part of his time at Braxton House, coming over the mountain only to visit the women and the Major from time to time; and he endured much in the endeavor to save his house from marauders. He had finally, in some collision of intemperate words, got into trouble with the Federal authorities and been carried away a prisoner to Alexandria. His absence had been a new and terrible stroke of calamity to Hetty, who soon made up her mind she was never to see him again. She in this new trouble gave up her thoughts to melancholy forebodings that dealt with the possibilities of her own removal, in one way or another, as the next thing to be looked for; and then what was to become of Phœbe, left with only Naomi and the Northern soldier in this mountain wilderness. In this train of thought Hetty was convinced that a wedding was itself a remedy, and therefore favored it.

As a trifle, a very swan's-down feather, will incline the nicely-balanced scale, even though it be weighing our destinies, perhaps it was a trifle that gave the last touch to this balance.

Phœbe was a good little Christian, yet she had some heathen fancies. Now, with the heathen religion is a very practical reality, and deity is a sort of universal bureau of information from which he can get answers to solve all doubts that are an impediment to action. He therefore practises divination. But do not his Christian brother and sister in fact imitate him in this? Are we not divining all the time by the interpretation of signs?

Naomi had foretold a death this year because in an apple-tree on the side of the mountain she had seen "wid her own eyes" nearly-ripe apples and blossoms at the same time.

But there is a kind of divination almost universal with the quiet country people; so common, indeed, that they practise it unconsciously. This is called by the learned *stichomancy*, or *sortes Virgiliani*. People open a volume, and the first passage that strikes the eye may be tortured into an advice, a command, or an answer to their thoughts, if even the remotest application can be perceived in the words to the case before them.

Upon serious occasions the volume used is the Holy Bible, and words that seem to have a perceptible relation to a subject of moment, if found in that reservoir of wise counsels, are accepted almost as if they really involved divine advice.

Apparently the reasoning is that the Bible is the sum of all wisdom ; that in it somewhere is counsel for man upon every phase of life ; and that when he needs this counsel and goes to this ready oracle to get it, the volume opens in his hands as if in answer to prayer at the very page that bears the counsel he needs. For those who believe all else that we are taught as religious truth there is not in this anything ridiculously incredible.

But this magic art is practised also with other books, and here even those who admit the force of a Biblical passage may be in doubt unless they know the plain fact that in country homes of thoughtful and sincere people every printed book is regarded with but little less reverence than the Bible itself, and is assumed to be the last form of human wisdom upon the subject with which it deals.

Now, there was at Skibbevan an old leather-bound folio volume of English poetry brought from England in the colonial days. Hiram had found it, scorched and wet, knocking around at the fire, and, recognizing it as a volume that the old doctor read a great deal, he had rescued it and brought it over the mountain as a great treasure.

Phœbe, in the last phase of her trouble, resorted to this grand old reservoir of wise thoughts and noble words.

In the silence of her chamber she said her prayers, then confidently opened the volume, and there

upon the fair top of the right-hand page was this
passage:

> "Open the temple-gates unto my love,—
> Open them wide that she may enter in ;
> And all the posts adorn as doth behove,
> And all the pillars deck with garlands trim,
> For to receive this saint with honor due
> That cometh in to you.
> Bring her to the high altar that she may
> The sacred ceremonies there partake
> The which do endless matrimony make,
> And let the roaring organs loudly play."

And thereupon Phœbe's face fell upon the page,
whiter, far whiter, than that time-stained record;
and she was like one dead.

Perhaps this was an ecstasy. All the saints had
ecstasies in the old times—a condition in which the
soul left the body, rambled awhile in other places,
and came home again; whereupon the saint arose
with the certainty that the impressions made upon
the soul in that hour were made by the touch of
deity. These things happened generally upon great
critical occasions; though Saint Catherine of Siena
went off in that way one day when she was roasting
mutton. But that, also, is a great critical occasion,
if the mutton is good.

However that may be, no saint ever arose from
her ecstasy with a firmer conviction that she was a
possessor of revealed truth than Phœbe upon this
occasion ; and I should like to know what dear little
woman in the same circumstances would not have

perceived in this grand tranquil commendation to the temple and to the marriage-ceremony a complete response to all Phœbe's thoughts, and the more complete because it was certainly the response she wished to receive.

And herein let us admire the excellence of the Chinese religion; for the Chinese, also, consult the deity in the way of divination, and if the answer is not the one they hoped for, they may repeat the trial again and again and again, and indefinitely. But if they once get the answer they want, deity itself commands that they shall not try again.

There are some facts in private life so particularly private that even the chronicler of our romantic experiences never gets much information about them; and it was this way with the simple ceremonies of the marriage of Phœbe Braxton to Major Pembroke. No secret was made of it at the time, to be sure; but, for reasons which the reader will presently hear about, there subsequently arose an apparent need for concealing all the details of that story, and little Phœbe was so successful in impressing upon the minds of the few witnesses the imperative need for secrecy that years afterwards, and when all the need for secrecy had passed away, they glued their lips together at the very mention of the subject—so inevitable is the effect of habit.

Perhaps my own curiosity on that subject has been most stirred by a point as to which the witnesses themselves could not have helped me—by what I may call, I suppose, the psychological part of the puzzle. How was it that when Pembroke had had so much of common knowledge, and even language itself, knocked out of him by the hard hits of that tough night on the mountain, he had enough knowledge of human relations left in him to know when to pop the question, and to know even that there was a question?

But that is a mystery we must all guess at. Perhaps this is knowledge so related to our primary human qualities that it can only be suppressed by the blow that ends life; or if this knowledge is overwhelmed, perhaps it is first in the race of recovery.

But it is certain, indeed, that Pembroke's memory of the past was unevenly affected, and that his recovery was consequently uneven; and in that inequality the more strictly natural conceptions of the mind, because related to a larger range of ideas, must have had an advantage.

CHAPTER XVII

THERE were blissful days at Skibbevan; and then upon the still air of that earthly paradise came a startling report. There had reached Winchester, it was said, a beautiful lady from the North, endeavoring to gain tidings of a lost husband whose name was Pembroke, and who was or had been a major in the Union army.

Hiram heard this story at the gatherings of the colored people in the valley; for as the lady had offered a reward for information of the lost one, and as it was known that there had been a wounded man at the mill, Hiram was asked often what his name was.

Presently news came that the lady at Winchester was assisted in her search by the Willoughbys and Gooches and other of Arthur's relations.

These families knew nearly all the facts of this history, but knew them vaguely. They had been scandalized by the report of Phœbe's marriage; and now that an opportunity came to get at all the details without seeming themselves to take the initiative in a painful inquiry, they encouraged and helped.

It is well known that the theory of our government in the war was that the States in rebellion were, as they had been from the first, component parts of our system, only that the operation of the laws was interrupted by insurrection; and that the supremacy of the law was to be restored as the government made progress in putting down resistance. Accepting this theory, the Gooches—Arthur's mother was of that family—said that if the officer who had married Phœbe Braxton was previously married in the North, he should be punished for bigamy if the authorities were sincere in their theory about the law. On our side it was thought that this was a good opportunity to demonstrate the sincerity of the government, and a regular prosecution was instituted.

Phœbe, as soon as she heard all this, was filled with consternation and dismay. As consternation implies that things generally are thrown down and cast into confusion, shuffled, jumbled, and left higgledy-piggledy, that was the state of her whole mind and soul; so that there was not a thought or fancy upon which she might lay hold as an anchor of hope of the position and safety of which she felt certain. Or she was like one who is in the field when the tipsy town is tumbled down by an earthquake, and no woman endeavoring to return home can tell which is her own doorway or fireside, or at what shrine she may pray without desecrating a sacred service.

And as the word *dismay* implies that the will, the sustaining force of human actions, is suddenly lost,—that the weakened nerves and muscles fall like loose ribbons for want of that which made them active parts of a vital unity,—so that word fitly states the sudden helplessness which came over the little lady.

But a sudden sweeping fire from the hot muzzles of destiny will weaken any line for a moment; yet if it is a good line it rallies again. And so Phœbe recovered herself, and she recovered only to open upon herself a new fire of reproaching; yet out of all this came, oddly enough, the salvation of the moment, for it indicated a direction in which to act, and to act was to satisfy some human need of her nature.

"She was to blame. She had married Pembroke; he had not married her. He had been absolutely unconscious of a past history; but she had known there was a past, and should have known all about it before she went so far, and then this trouble would not have come upon him."

For she did not once conceive of this trouble save as it was a calamity to him. That it was the ruin of the beautiful hope of the Braxtons did not occur to her.

And then came a sweeter thought.

"Well, at least her Pembroke was a new man. At least in his soul, in his mind, there was no other wife. It was hers, and hers alone; but alas! the strange cruelty of destiny, that the body which was also the property of the other Pembroke who had been married in Maine should be responsible to justice for acts done in a new life! But how would the justice of that far-away past life know what had been done in this new, remote, isolated existence? Then a thought flashed through her mind that justice must have evidence; and she understood what Hiram had said about "looking for evidence," and she asked herself what evidence there was of Pembroke's marriage with her.

"There is the record at the little church."

Another thought which greatly troubled Phœbe was that it might not be intended really to arrest the Major. She knew the names of the men who had been sent on this errand as infamous for some relation to every act of lawlessness and brigandage ever done in the country, and she no sooner heard these names than the fancy flashed across her thought that the real purpose was to pretend to arrest the Major, to provoke him to resistance, and to kill him while resisting the officers.

That, she believed, would please the Willoughbys.

Phœbe nevertheless thought that, as there might be a real intention to try the Major, her first duty was to him, and her first act should be to make it difficult to convict him if they caught him; though she intended they should not catch him if she could help it.

Now, the most certain evidence of the marriage was the record kept in the little church. By destroying that she would destroy, it is true, the record that her own side of her relation to the Major was honorable, but she would destroy what might prove him guilty of a crime. If it did not appear before the judges at Warrenton or Winchester or elsewhere that she was married to the Major, it would appear that she had lived in illicit relations with him. She was ready for whatever consequences might come to her if she could save him.

And with all this thought and worry and wonder, went side by side, and playing in and out and around, like airs upon other instruments in an orchestra, a fear that the trial and what might come of it was not the worst before her.

If there was a trial, there would at least be justice, and the Major's condition would be taken into account. She never imagined that ordinary courts would raise the eyebrows of incredulity over such a story. She could not comprehend that any would doubt what she knew so well.

But she feared what might happen if Pembroke, brought into the presence of this lady from the North, should remember and know her. How cold had been the life between them Phœbe did not know. They had loved one another, she assumed; and if an earlier claim to Pembroke's love was good now, what would become of her?

At midnight two women left the old mill at Skibbevan. One was Phœbe, the other Agate.

It was not, apparently, a perilous trip from the old mill to the little chapel. No wild beasts infested that region, nor were there any demons or witches of romance there. Yet there was more danger in the journey than either of these women thought, for

13

there were armies in the valley, and the mountain was a place of refuge for scores of armed ragamuffins, half soldiers and half highwaymen.

But they went safely through all that. As in a crowd if you see one you know and fix your gaze upon him he is well-nigh sure to see you, while if you turn your eyes away you are very apt to pass unseen, so it almost appeared that their very unconsciousness of the proximity of enemies kept the enemies unconscious of them.

Phœbe had not all the way a thought of danger. Her mind was not sufficiently free for such a mere personal indulgence as the sense of fear. She was too intent upon the purpose before her to consider the possible accidents of the way. But Agate, who had not the inspiration of such a purpose, and had all the superstitious nature of her race, saw ghosts and devils at every step.

Thus it happened that the delicate lady led the way without a thought of present evil, while there went trembling behind her the strong slave, who in the presence of any real enemy would have fought for her comrade with the courage and tenacity of a she-lion.

They reached the church, and captured the heavy volume they sought; and the next consideration was what should be done with it. One might suppose that this doubt had been determined by the way; but in truth women seldom undertake an enterprise with their minds made up as to all the points; and though Phœbe had in her mind the general purpose

to put this book beyond the possibility of use as
evidence, she had not made up her mind how to destroy it, nor thought how its destruction could be
accomplished.

Now, this volume contained the only evidence
that her relations to Pembroke were those of honest
matrimony, so far as she knew, and this would have
made it sacred in most women's eyes; but it did
not in hers, for was it not a document that might
prove Pembroke guilty of a crime?

The thought, therefore, that this was the only
record of her marriage did not save the volume; but
the thought that did save it was that it contained
the record of the marriages of many other women,
and that she had no right to imperil the welfare of
others when this was not absolutely necessary to
save her own.

So between them they carried the heavy volume
away and hid it in a secure crevice in a rocky recess
of the mountain.

Then they hurried away homeward, this time
with the speed of fear; for now Phœbe was conscious
of a guilty act.

That night there was something in the air that
made it difficult for any one at Skibbevan to be at
rest. How it is that the state of one mind or
soul can without any apparent personal communication act upon another mind or soul the philoso-
phers do not know; but the fact is one of experience, and I am not sure that it is more difficult
than a score of other facts. Our very diseases have

such an effect upon the atmosphere near us that
they who breathe the same air get the same mala-
dies; and a storm in one soul, though concealed, may
so affect the atmosphere as to convey that mood to
another soul sympathetically related to this one.

Pembroke sat in the little piazza in the drowsy
air of the night filled with the rhythmical noises of
the swinging vines and swinging trees; sat and
waited for Phœbe, who, busy, as he supposed, at
some other part of the old home, would come to him
soon.   She seemed to him to be away longer than
usual; but this did not strike him as strange, did
not ruffle the delightful tranquillity of the patience
with which he waited.   And as he so waited, soothed
by all the voices of the night, the honey-heavy dew
of slumber settled upon his senses.

Suddenly he started from this sleep, and whether
he had slept five minutes or as many hours he could
not tell; but he was wide awake, and filled with a
definite consciousness that there was something
wrong on foot.   But what was it?   Where was
Phœbe?   It must relate to her.

He went about and could not find Phœbe.
Through the various parts of the old place all was
still; apparently everybody slept.   But Phœbe was
gone.   Gone whither?   Gone for what purpose?
Gone for how long?

He wandered in and out of the different rooms
with these thoughts coming and going in his mind,
and his trouble grew almost to a panic.

And then the habit of trusting her asserted itself.

How had she been safe in all these days and nights, to
be in danger now merely because she was out of his
sight? This did not altogether calm him, but it
lightened the strain and kept him tranquil for a
time; and then as the fever of fear began to come
again, he heard the light step of Phœbe on the piazza, and in a second they were face to face.

He saw her trouble as she saw his.

And then she told him in a few swift words
where she had been and what she had done.

But why had she done that? Why was it necessary?

Phœbe felt like one who stands beside an abyss
into which it is his duty to plunge, as she thought
in one short second how much there was that he did
not know, and how imperative it was that all
should be told this very moment.

And then she began to tell him. But he did not
understand; and she had to stop and reflect where
she should begin her story, so that it would connect
with the point at which his new mental life began.

"Skibbevan was not your first home," she said,
"and we were not your first friends."

He only looked placidly at her and waited for her
to go on, as if perhaps such a thought had already
occurred to him and he had no curiosity in regard
to it.

"Before that you were hurt."

He put his hand to his head unconsciously.

"Yes," she said, "your head; and we thought
for many months that you would die. But in your

recovery you did not regain the memory of your past life. We never liked to say much about it; we did not know what effect it might have. But now it is necessary to tell it."

"Necessary for what reason?" he said.

"Because you have to go away."

"Away from here!" he said; "from you! Impossible! I cannot do it. I cannot comprehend that there can be any reason for it."

"But there is. Men have come from the North to arrest you. They say that when we were married you committed a crime, because you had another wife."

"Another wife!" he said.

"Yes; in the beforetime."

"Another wife—in the beforetime;" and he repeated these words mechanically over and over again, and then sat silently with a strange gaze in his eyes, as if some recovered intimations of an intellectual pathway into the past had started his will upon the strange endeavor to find in his brain points of connection by which to aid his exploration.

"They call her," said Phœbe, with hesitation—"they call her Lætitia."

He started to his feet as if that word had touched the key of some magnetic battery connected with explosive substances in the cells of his brain, and as if that explosion had blown away the curtain that hid the past.

Phœbe half rose as he started away, and then, unable to regain her feet, sank lower, and her head sank almost to her knees, and she rested there in abject misery, for she did not know that the impulse which that word had stirred was one of repulsion—was an act of instinctive aversion to all with which that name was associated; and she listened to her fears, and thought it was a movement away from her.

He strode up and down the little room with an energy strange to him then; and then returning, gathered her up in his strong arms, folded her tenderly to his bosom, and said softly:

"Phœbe, my love, my only darling!" And then they wept together, and he said, "How was I hurt? How did I come here?"

"You were hurt in a battle. You came as a soldier."

"Yes, that is it," he said. "Where is the regiment—and old Dave? My God! how long has it been?"

"You were left for dead on the field of battle. I saved you—Papa and Aunt Hetty, and Agate and I. You were reported dead. But she has denied it, and has done this."

Then there was an interval of tears and caresses, and she said:

"Pretended officers have left Winchester to capture you. They are not officers, they are some of the mountain ruffians, and if they find you here they will murder you. You must leave before it is light."

"Phœbe," he said, "I do not altogether understand it; but you, who do, must guide me as to what is best for your welfare and for my honor."

"No evil menaces me," she said.

"Why, then," he said, "the regiment—"

"Here," she said, "is the regiment."

And with a step away she opened the door of a closet nearly hidden in the wall, and showed his uniform, brushed and carefully hung there with the scrupulous nicety with which a little girl would put up her first Sunday bonnet.

At the sight of the blue cloth, the buttons, and, above all, at the sight of the sabre hanging by the belt beside the coat, he was excited so that he trembled for a moment and leaned upon Phœbe; who in her turn was frightened, and thought despite the long delay all this had at last been made known too soon—that his brain was not yet sufficiently recovered to stand the shock of these disclosures.

"It is too much to endure," she said. "It was wrong to tell you yet."

"No," he answered, "it was right. I understand it now."

Thereupon he reached for the sabre, and taking it down drew it from the scabbard, and grasped the hilt firmly as if to balance the weight of the blade against the strength of his wrist; and then, perhaps because some electrical influence went from that bit of steel into the man, his nerves grew steady, he was calm, and in that instant appeared to recover a full consciousness of all those facts of his life to which the weapon was related. It was as if it needed that weight in his hand to make him himself once more.

"Yes, Phœbe," he said, "you are right. I must go away."

And then Phœbe, who had been sustained by the thought of the duty to be done, and now saw only the loss before her, went down upon her knees and prayed; and Pembroke knelt speechlessly beside her, only putting his hand upon her head as if with the wish that he might be included in the benefit of those sweet prayers.

CHAPTER XVIII.

Before daylight Skibbevan was as much abandoned as any of the homes one saw in Virginia in those days when naught was left but two melancholy chimneys—the timber parts burned away, and only the masonry remaining in monumental remembrance of what had been. Skibbevan was left intact; not a scrap of furniture displaced. But if the home had been burned away, the spot could scarcely have looked more desolate than the sun saw it that day when late in the forenoon he had climbed high enough to peep over the crest of the mountains at that scene of so much recent bliss. But the sun has observed so much like that since he has been upon his travels that he has no longer any feeling for the pathos of it.

Phœbe and Aunt Hetty, Naomi and Agate, were to be immediately hidden at a secure place in the hills, and Hiram was to accompany the Major for a way till he should put him upon a sure path up the valley, that he might reach the army. Then Hiram was to return, guide the women to a yet deeper recess of the mountains, and, by keeping up a regular communication with Skibbevan, minister to their daily wants. His courage and sagacity were

accepted as sure guarantees that no one would capture him; or if they did, that he would not be a useful witness.

There was a heart-breaking farewell between
Phœbe and the Major at the place where the wom-
en were to leave the route,—in which, however, they
restrained themselves because of the presence of
the others; and then the two groups started away
rapidly upon their different journeys; Phœbe for-
getting, in her anxiety that he should escape this
immediate peril, the many other perils that were before him; and he somewhat distracted from this
present loss by the feeling of an imperative sense
of his duty elsewhere.

Hiram and the Major tramped resolutely onward
all the forenoon, seeing not a soul, and at midday
lunched and rested.

Hiram improved this occasion to show off a little
before the Major, with a kind of natural vanity flow-
ing from some military impulses in his nature, his
dexterity with the remarkable weapon he carried,
which had excited in the Major only a speechless
curiosity.

This weapon was Hiram's own contrivance, and
was very nearly a country blacksmith's reproduction
of an ancient bill. Upon the smaller extremity of
a staff made from an ash sapling was fastened the
blade of one of those short stiff scythes called brush-
hooks, and this blade was ground to a point in such
a way as to remove entirely the forward bend in the
blade.

Now, the staff was about twelve feet long, and of such a size in the butt that it could have been handled only with exertion by anybody without the giant shoulders, arms, and hands of Hiram—to whom, indeed, it seemed as light as a willow switch.

With this weapon, and rushing one or two steps, he could strike, with deadly aim every time, his own hat suspended in the branches at a point twenty-five feet from where he stood.

"Could you strike a man that way?" said the Major.

"Sure enough, Massa Major, I can do dat," he said; "and if dese fellows gives half a chance, I show yer. Dey talk about ole Virginny; and I'm as good ole Virginny as any of 'em."

It was more than an hour past noon when they started forward again, striking immediately and without the need of agreement in words into the steady long stride of men who feel that the distance before them bears an unsatisfactory relation to the time in which they wish to put it behind them. As neither of them had that merry heart which is said to go all the day,—and one of them certainly had the sad heart which, on the same authority, "tires in a mile, O"—this want and this weight were equally overcome by the resolute spirit that neither was without.

Suddenly Hiram, who was a few paces ahead, as showing the way, stopped short, bolt upright in the road, and said:

"What's dat, Major?"

" What ?" said Pembroke.

" Don't yer hear a noise ?"

Pembroke listened, but heard no sound save the little movement of the rustling leaves; but even that noise was never fainter than now, for there was not breeze enough to stir the heavy tree-tops, and there were no lower branches here, as there seldom are in the dense forest. But as their senses were thus kept on the alert for a minute, there came upon the still air a faint harsh noise, more like the protest of a rusty hinge than like any sound peculiar to the wild hillside.

" Perhaps some rusty well-wheel in the valley," said the Major.

" Major," said Hiram, with the confidence of superior knowledge, " dere ain't no well-wheel for ten miles. People on de mountain gets water out of de branches; and down in de valley dey draws wid a well-sweep. Dat's de rusty wheel of some ole nigger's mule-cart; but what ole nigger's comin' on de mountain wid a mule-cart dese times ? Dat's what I'm wonderin' at."

Now, Hiram's imagined familiarity with the sound he heard caused it to excite his wonder rather than his fear, otherwise his half-Indian instincts would have caused him to hide at once; and had he done so, they would have viewed from some safe lookout near by what they presently saw, but would have missed the notable experiences of that day.

For scarcely had Hiram delivered his opinion on the noise than there came in sight around a sharp

turn in the road, two hundred yards away, a spectacle strange to Pembroke, but apparently not altogether strange, though startling, to Hiram.

"Dat's a nigger funeral," he said; "but what
nigger is it? Didn't hear any one was dead."

There was a rickety old open wagon drawn by a
mule, driven by a colored woman closely veiled,
who sat up at the front of the wagon, while behind
her in the wagon was what might well be a coffin
covered with a black cloth, and in the road walked,
in couples, following the wagon, four colored
women closely veiled.

"Lors a massy!" said Hiram, "what nigger can
dis be? And every one of dem culled women's six
foot high; and where did dey borry so many veils
dese times? Come on, Major." And Hiram, with
a sudden air of resolution which told the Major that
it was a moment in which to be on his guard, started
ahead, and they walked side by side swiftly toward
the advancing cortege, each prepared for a ready
use of weapons. Now, this advance was more fortunate than Hiram knew, for it gave to the funeral
party the impression that others were on the road
behind Hiram and the Major; and more surprised
than our friends were, and not knowing what to
expect, these five uncommonly tall colored women
kept steadily on their way.

"How dey do step out!" muttered Hiram as they
came near; and indeed as the gait of our acquaint-
ances was a good one, and the pace of the others
not at all that of women who are lingering on their

last journey with a friend, the two parties passed without a word exchanged, within two or three minutes of the time they first caught sight of each other.

"Dey ain't neighborly niggers," said Hiram. "Not a word, eh? Dat's mighty queer. Dar's some shecoonery in dis."

Now, Hiram's state of mind was a very odd one. Like all men of his race, his perceptions were very acute, and he thus discovered at the first glimpse,— "with half an eye," as the people say,—that there was something wrong about that funeral. Those women were all too tall; they strode forward with a free use of their feet not characteristic of persons used to wearing petticoats. They were too much veiled, and they were not sociable enough. Besides, if any colored person was dead in all that region, would he not have heard of it? Yet, though he discerned readily, he reasoned slowly, and did not reach over-hastily the thought that perhaps it was not a funeral, nor yet the inquiry, if it was not a funeral, what was it?

His instincts were right, however, though his reason was slow; for the moment that little turn in the road put them out of sight of the others, making a sudden sign to the Major, he started on a hard run, and the Major followed. At this place the road wound a great deal on account of the irregularities of the mountain-side and the need of skirting many steep, rocky places; consequently the view up or down the road was not open for any distance, and Hiram, understanding that the others, if they returned, must be nearly upon their heels before they could see them, thus obtained five or six minutes' grace in which to choose an ambush.

He had apparently fixed upon the place as he ran; for, coming to a point at which a smaller road cut off from that they were on and descended the mountain, he ran forward beyond a heavy mass of boulders that stood in the angle of these two roads, and, dashing behind the boulders, made his way by a rough crevice back to the face of the mass, where, in an open space covered from the front by a dense growth of vines and brushwood, they could, unseen and unheard, looking down upon the road, both see and hear.

By this time, Pembroke, reasoning that if those they had just passed were not what they seemed,—if they were persons in disguise,—they were probably on some evil errand, and might be those enemies who were reported on the way to capture him, became uneasy lest they should not return; for if they went on, what danger might there not be for Phœbe?

"Are these the fellows from Winchester?" he said to Hiram.

"Dat's it, suah, Major; dat's it, suah. Dat mus' be it: never reckoned dat. Dese am de fellows from Winchester. Fixed demselves up like culled wumen so de Linkum sojers wouldn't stop 'em."

"What will they do now?"

"Dey'll stop in de road dere, and reckon dis ting

a little, and den dey'll come for us, because you're
de man dey want.   But dey'll come mighty shy,
and somebody'll be all mommicked up 'fore night.
Are you all ready ?"

The Major had his sabre-hilt near his hand, and
had his revolver in his belt; but the cartridges were
now so old that he did not know whether he could
count upon them.

He was as ready, however, as it was possible to
be in the circumstances, and they waited in silence.

Waiting in that way for the enemy to come—
waiting in a reasonably good ambush for an inevitable conflict with an overwhelming number, in
which it must depend upon your skill to make two
men equal to five—is a thing that men get used to
in war; but it makes untried men impatient, and
stirs the old fellows to be sure not to act precipitately,
yet not to let the right moment go by.

Hiram had been right as to what the others would
do; for in a few minutes one figure, one tall fellow
dressed in butternut cloth—this time without petticoats or veil, and with a rifle ready before him—appeared in the road at the first turn in the direction
from which our friends had come.   Seeing the way
clear before him, he made a sign to those behind
him, and hurried forward toward the next turn.

"If dey don't move faster dan dat, we could 'a'
run clean away from dem, Major," said Hiram.

"But it is better this way," said the Major.
"They might return and pursue the women."

This was hardly said before the advance man was

14

in the road beside the Major and Hiram; and as he could see down both ways and did not know which road to take, he waited for the others. If the Major had been sure of his cartridges, he would have closed the career of this fellow now, and thus have had one fewer to deal with; but the fall of a hammer that did not explode the cartridge would not hurt the foe, and would betray the hidden two, and they would have been presently shot to death in the hole in which they lay.

To fire upon him was therefore a risk not to be taken, and the Major held his hand.

Presently the others joined the man who had already arrived, and the five—all of the same sort, rough customers in butternut, such as always live upon the skirts of an army, and are fonder of all things else pertaining to strife than the smell of gunpowder—held a council of war in the road.

"Reckon we've lost 'em," said one.

"How could we lose 'em?" said another.

"We uns has been durn foolish about this," said a third. "If we'd followed their tracks in the road from where they started to run, we'd 'a' had somethin' to lead us to jist where they're at."

"Well, now, Jim," said the first fellow in butternut, "nobody can't please you. Soon as I seen by the tracks there that they'd started to run, I sez to myself, 'If we stop to look for tracks, they'll get to the Yankee army before we can ketch 'em;' and that's the reason I went fast. Can't follow no tracks and run, too."

Hereupon one who had been down the by-road returned, and reported that he could not find any traces of footsteps that way.

Fortunately for our friends in the crevices of the boulders, these five had upon their advance halted at this very spot, and between the mule and the wagon and their own shuffling about there was such a confusion of traces that they did not even endeavor to follow any footprint up the main road, but, concluding hastily that, as there were no traces the other way, they must have gone by the wagon-road, determined to push rapidly forward in that direction.

"Well, as the little road comes into the wagon-road again a ways ahead," said the leader, "we can cover more ground by some going each way."

"But he's a tough-looking fellow," said the one called Jim; "not much sick man about him; and that Hiram Braxton ain't a baby; and dividing our forces ain't a good plan with sich as them."

"Well, we won't be far away," said the first, "and a shot in either road could fetch up the others."

"Jist as yer like," was the answer.

So two went one way and three the other. And Jim, who went with the three, called out as parting advice:

"Kill him if yer see him. There ain't no other chance."

And then the two lying perdu heard them dispute, and, though they could not see clearly all the time, got glimpses occasionally which assured them of a clear road for the moment.

Now, Hiram, whose duty was to get the Major safely on his way, was for waiting till these fellows were well advanced, and for then following for a certain distance the road taken by the two and leaving it by a way he knew, and getting into the wet region at the foot of the mountain. But the Major, thinking all the time of Phœbe and of what these fellows might do if disappointed, did not want to disappoint them entirely.

"We have got the advantage," he said, "in knowing their plan, and in knowing that they are divided; and if we could get at the two before they reach the others, we could give a good account of ourselves."

"Dat can be done, Major," said Hiram, "if must be."

"How?" said the Major.

"Dis yeah path dat dem two fellows went is mighty crooked; winds away mile and a half, and comes back to de boulders 'bout half a mile from here. It's mighty rough, but we can get dar 'fore dey do."

"Forward, then," said the Major; "that's our chance."

So they scrambled out of the lucky refuge to which they had taken, and jumped and fell and climbed and slid onward toward Hiram's strategic point. It was a mighty rough way, as Hiram had said, and the Major went down so badly two or three times that Hiram thought he had a man with a broken leg on his hands; but they reached the place, and in good time, as it proved.

Pembroke planned an ambush upon the theory that the two foes coming with a little care, but not with a great deal, and much as he had seen them all come up to the point where he was last hidden, would advance on this narrow path one some yards in advance of the other. He placed himself nearest to the advancing enemy, and Hiram at a place about ten paces farther up the path.

His plan was to let the first man—the one with the rifle—pass him, and then as the other came opposite him to kill this one with a pistol-shot, which, indeed, from the place where the Major was hidden would be fired from a point so near the man that the shot could not but be fatal if the cartridge was good.

It was assumed that at this shot the man with the rifle would wheel round and endeavor to get a shot at the Major; and as he should turn, Hiram, who would be behind him, was to come upon him with his bill.

But the Major's pistol might miss fire on account of the age of the cartridges.

In that case the Major was to close with his man so that the other could not fire without danger of hitting his friend; and while he hesitated, Hiram's bill was to come into play, and then, if all went well, they would be two to one.

But not even so little a battle as this is ever fought precisely as it is planned.

Both men came stepping forward swiftly, but on the alert, and in the order imagined. Pembroke fired as had been planned, and the cartridge was good and his man fell; but the other did not turn. On the contrary, getting somehow over his shoulder a lightning-like glimpse of what had happened, he started and ran like a deer straight up the path, with Hiram at his heels; for Hiram, having got his part of the programme definitely in his head, could not change in a hurry the conception that it was his duty to hit this fellow. He gained upon him enough to make a thrust that caught the fellow, but very lightly, on one side of his neck; at which touch the fellow dashed away out of the path, and, luckily for Hiram, the vines and branches caught his rifle, jerked it from any chance for an aim, and he, seeing Hiram so near, dropped it and scrambled forward in his desperate flight.

But seeing suddenly that Hiram's weapon was caught in the vines, and supposing, apparently, that the vines would hold Hiram long enough to give him a chance for a shot, he struggled forward and stooped for his rifle. But he had not counted upon the length of Hiram's weapon. Hiram, pushing his way only half into the thicket, with one desperate thrust drove the scythe into the fellow's back, over his shoulder, as he was stooping, and he never rose. Then Hiram struggled forward and got the rifle himself, and got from the body of the prostrate man about twenty cartridges.

Then the Major got the revolver and cartridges

of the other, who was hit in the head, and they were well supplied with arms and ammunition.

"I was possessed to do it," said Hiram; "I was possessed to do it! But, sure's yer born, Major, I reckoned I'd missed a figure when I seen him run dat way."

"You did it well, Hiram," said the Major. "You did it like a good and brave soldier."

And Hiram's face shone like a patch of varnished wall where the sun touches it.

But the shot fired would be taken by the others as the signal for them, and they would be on hand very shortly; and what was to be done next?

Pembroke, seeing how little these fellows had been up to this sort of fighting, and believing the others might be as easily caught, wanted to lie in wait for them also; but Hiram was against this because it was not likely that five together should be without one or two more skilled in bushwhacking, and he believed in the choice of new ground.

Pembroke, therefore, yielding to the opinion that the women would certainly be safe before these fellows, taking care of their wounded and burying their dead, could proceed to Skibbevan, even if now inclined to go there, and conceding that they could fight to more advantage on ground of their own selection if pursued, accepted Hiram's plan.

They therefore started boldly backward upon the path by which the others had come, in order not to leave it in the vicinity of this conflict, though not knowing but the three on the other road might come this way.

At about half a mile from the place at which the dead man lay in the path, Hiram suddenly quitted it by a turn to the left hand, and stepping into the bed of a mountain-torrent, dry at this time, led the way down the mountain by a very steep and difficult zigzag.

They went on thus for an hour without a word and hearing not a sound from their late pursuers, and now began to find the way easy and sloping into broad reaches of nearly level woodland.

CHAPTER XIX.

POTLUCK.

THEY heard no more of their foes, and all the rest of that day saw not a sign of the existence in the mountain of any human creature. Late in the afternoon they were upon wet ground, in a sort of half-swampy region near the river, and in the dim light at nightfall Hiram led the way through a deep swamp where any but one familiar with the path would have been mired at every step; and so they reached a dry knoll in this hidden place, which, it immediately occurred to the Major, was perhaps a station on the "underground railroad." There they ate heartily of Naomi's provender, and passed the night as little disturbed as if it had been in the garden of Eden.

Next day they finished Naomi's supply and got an early start. They reached the river before noon, and Hiram, leading the Major, hunted up and down the stream to find what he evidently knew was there, but could not readily discover. Eventually he returned, poling a rickety old skiff, in which, together, they reached the other side, partly by help of the pole and partly by the current, which, carrying them swiftly downstream, carried them across, thanks to a bend in the river.

Here was the end of Hiram's service, for the road that the Major was to take was plain and clear from this point, and ran not more than three or four hundred yards from where they stood. They parted at the skiff, with that full-hearted grasp of the hand that is exchanged only between men who have some good reason to deeply know each other's nature.

Hiram's eyes glistened with joy as the Major said :

"Hiram, I feel safer about the women since I've seen how you can use your weapon."

"Mars'r Major, if any of 'em comes dar, I'll jab it into 'em! I'll jab it into 'em!"

This was said with an energy that almost upset the little skiff as the current carried her out down the next reach of the river.

Pembroke went steadily on in the direction that had been indicated by Hiram; and at every step almost gained the assurance that he was approaching a very large encampment, for he could hear an occasional drum-beat and a bugle-call, and the screaming of many mules. But he could not for a great while get even a glimpse of the country before him, because he was so far down in the level of the valley that the heavy timber completely obscured the view of things beyond.

For hours he pushed on, however, and, except for the birds and squirrels, saw not a sign of life in the woods about him; and the foliage of the tall trees was so dense that the day grew dim, and it seemed to be already near nightfall, when it was probably only about the middle of the afternoon. He was in the neutral belt that surrounds an active army—too near to it for the enemy's guerillas, but too far away to happen upon foragers, unless it had been an organized foraging expedition.

He now changed his direction, in the hope to get more speedily into the open valley, feeling the certainty that as the base of the army near to which he now knew he was must be at Winchester, he would, upon the by-roads nearer the turnpike, come upon some stragglers who had wandered off from the line of march, and who would have food.

In fact, this change brought him out of the heavy timber and upon an open ridge, from which he got a glimpse of the country and some indications of the camp, but uncertain through the woods, in the valley itself.

His most immediate purpose, however, was attained. He came upon a soldier, a fine strapping fellow, who was stepping out well on a kind of farmers' wood-road that ran along the timber at right angles with the path by which Pembroke had now come out of the woods, and which consequently led toward the point from which the bugle-calls came. The Major was at a point which the soldier would reach in a few moments, and he waited; and the soldier came on with the step, not of a straggler, but of one who wishes to get into camp.

As the soldier came within a rod, his eye caught the figure of a man, and he halted and brought his piece up; but as a more direct scrutiny showed the uniform, he dropped the butt of his rifle to the ground and saluted the Major.

"Where are you from?" said the Major.

"Hospital at Winchester, sir; wounded at Opequan; recovered, sent forward to join my regiment. Perhaps you can show me the way, sir?"

"No," said the Major. "I was wounded also, and have been hidden in the mountains here a great while, and want to get to the camp myself. But I am a little used up and hungry."

"Yes, sir; you are pale, not quite right yet, sir. Please to sit there." And he partly supported and partly pushed the Major down upon a comfortable tuft of grass at the root of a large tree.

Then he dropped his knapsack, blanket, and haversack, carefully rested his rifle on the accumulation of his kit, ran two or three rods away to a little vein of water he had just passed, returned with his tin cup half-full of water, and, as he came forward again, tipped out of his canteen into the cup a good pull of whiskey, and passed it to the Major, who speedily put the whole draught where it would do most good.

"That will stiffen you up until you can eat, sir."

Then the soldier brought out of the recesses of his bag a little store, which he had evidently laid away for his own comfort, of the dainty light biscuit for the making and baking of which the kitchen Dinah possesses some secret, and which are a grateful variation from the monotony of hard-tack, as

well as a grand inducement for a soldier to get on
a by-road, since on the main road where the whole
army is no given number of darky women could
make enough for all; but one soldier on a by-road
is sure to obtain this tribute of African hero-worship
and gratitude.

These little cakes had been split open while
warm, and a space between them filled with that
honey of the Shenandoah Valley of which nobody
knows much but the people of the valley, and which
nobody has fully appreciated at its true merits but a
soldier who has campaigned in that country. In the
rush of the Major's appetite these dainties melted
away like snowflakes on a hot gun, and the generous
fellow who had turned out his treasure for an officer
in distress said :

"These will do till we find something more sub-
stantial."

As the Major thanked the soldier for his happy
supply of provender and the good-will with which
he gave it, they fell into conversation, and it was
agreed that they should proceed together in accord-
ance with a plan the soldier already had in mind, to
cover yet before nightfall about half the distance
between them and the camp, have supper, bivouac
on the hills, and, starting at sunrise, get into camp
early next day.

Refreshed by the soldier's whiskey and cakes, the
Major was soon ready, and they went ahead at a
good gait. He was a stout fellow, the comrade
thus found—a well-constructed youngster, with a

handsome, smooth face, blue eyes, and of ready speech; and from him, without showing altogether his want of acquaintance with recent military operations, the Major learned that the army then in the valley, and commanded by Sheridan, was in camp near the head of the valley, on a tributary of the Shenandoah called Cedar Creek; and that the Major's regiment was there in an organization now entitled the Sixth Corps, which had been formed since the Major was wounded.

Even the name of Sheridan was new to the Major, for it had not been heard much in the East at the time he was knocked over; and as he heard the soldier name with pride that glorious fighting organization, the Sixth Corps, he discovered that he had some small share in its glory, for though its name was new, yet his regiment, brigade, and division were part of it, though formerly they had been in the Fourth Corps under General Keyes.

More in a dream than in the full possession of his senses,—in a whirl with the recent recovery of so many impressions,—the Major toward the last simply gave himself up to the guidance of the soldier, and followed without a word, until they suddenly came to a halt in a poor little inclosure that served for a farm-yard, and the Major looked up to observe the soldier holding a colloquy with the farmer.

The soldier was trying to buy some choice morsel of meat or bread to feed the Major, and the farmer said:

"We're just eat out clean, and hain't got a

mouthful"—which was the ordinary and indeed very natural refrain of the time and the place.

There were hens scratching around, and the soldier said:

"What will you take for one of them hens?"

"Well, now, I can't sell none o' them hens. They're the last I've got; and when the Confederate army was to Winchester and 'bout hyar, I could 'a' sold 'em all for two dollars and a half a piece."

"Secesh money?"

"Ye-es; but I don't want to sell 'em for any kind of money."

Just then a gun went off, and a hen that, in the confidence of home habits, had strayed within three or four yards of the muzzle of the soldier's piece sprawled and kicked her last kick on the ground.

"Now, farmer," said the soldier, "that one ain't much use to you, and I'll give you a dollar for her —good money, too. You see I'm fond of chicken, and here's a wounded officer that's used up and wants a good feed; so we can't stand on as much ceremony as is customary."

Thereupon the soldier passed out his dollar; and though the farmer clutched the money eagerly enough, he was inclined to continue his complaint.

"Never mind," said the soldier. "You pocket the money, old man, and if you can get a dollar for every chicken you've got left, my advice is, take it. They give us now four days' rations to last five days; and that means to live on the country for one day, and it's my opinion we do a little more. Sheri-

dan's ordered to clear out this valley now so that
the Secesh can't come down it again, and he'll do
it. So don't mourn over this chicken, but save
your tears for greater occasions."

Thereupon the soldier and the Major stepped out
again on their journey; and when well on the road
once more, the soldier said :

"Like as not there was two or three of these
guerilla fellows hid away in that shanty, so it won't
do to stop near here or they'll be on us in the
night; though we may have reinforcements when
we make a fire, for there's a good many of our fellows in the Varmount brigade that's just like me;
that is, their time was out two or three days ago,
and they've enlisted again and are going to the front.
They're out on all the by-roads, having a nice tramp
for fun."

It was about an hour later that, as they forded a
pretty deep run, the soldier found an abandoned
camp-kettle, which he at once seized.

"That's the daisy," he said; "and we might as
well halt now, for this will be troublesome to carry."

So they halted, on the knoll that they mounted as
they left the stream, under a wide-branched, dense-
ly-leaved white-pine tree. Here the soldier soon
made a glorious fire, and also a shelter, for the Octo-
ber night was now nearly upon them, and the north
wind, blowing up the valley, somewhat open at this
point, whistled sharply over this exposed point,
even though they were over on the southern slope.

From the abundance of dry wood near, the soldier fed the fire; and bringing the camp-kettle about half full of water, built it upon a good foundation of stones placed like a tripod, so that it might not tip over at a critical moment.

Having made the fire and put on the kettle, he skyugled around for some distance and came upon a bit of ancient snake-fence, the division-line, perhaps, of two estates, and brought on his shoulder half a dozen stakes from this; and these he placed with one end in the ground and the other against a long, low branch of the pine; and when his rubber blanket was fastened on the windward side of this barrier, there was a complete defence against the sharp wind.

At the same time the Major had kept the fire lively, and cleanly plucked the old hen. Scarcely was this much of preparation completed when it was made plain that the soldier was right in his anticipations about company, for another soldier joined them, and, with an easy "How are you, partner?" to the soldier and a salute to the Major, sat himself down at a little distance from the fire.

His eyes were suddenly riveted upon the hen, fat, round, and ancient, plucked and singed as she lay on the oil-cloth flap of the soldier's haversack.

"Partner," he said to the soldier, "that was a layin' hen."

"Was it?" said the other.

"Yes. Will you sell the eggs? Her wattles shows she's got some."

15

" Wattles, eh ?"

" Yes."

"Well, what'll you give for 'em ?" said the other, who, though generous enough to divide with all the world, met a commercial proposition in a commercial spirit, and recognized in the new-comer one who should have been a contractor.

"Now," said the last man, who was from Massachusetts, "I've got some nice sweet butter."

"Done," said Vermont.   "Pass out your butter. But you take the chance on the eggs."

"Oh yes," said the other; and the old hen was soon ripped open and Massachusetts was happy, for there were really in her eggs of all sizes and every degree of advancement, from one with a shell about half formed down to tiny ones the size of a buckshot.   There must have been about twenty very near the size of bullets.

From this moment a good meal was perceptible ; for Vermont had some hard bread left, there was butter now, and the old hen was put in the pot.   Massachusetts balanced his tin cup on the edge of the fire and boiled his eggs, and they sat down around the cheery blaze and bubble, and while they were musing the fire burned.

Every pause is not awful.   Sometimes there is a pleasant tranquillity of spirit between comrades beside a fire that crackles, which needs not words for sympathy of soul.

But they fell into conversation as Massachusetts drew out his eggs and for courtesy passed them around on a piece of bark, each of the others taking one of the little yellow bullets, not enough to encroach upon the supply, but sufficient as an acknowledgment of the politeness.

"By Jiminy!" said Vermont, "it's lucky we didn't open that hen by the farm-house. Old Secesh would have wanted another dollar. He'd 'a' counted every one of them as eggs, and then counted every egg as a chicken; and so they would 'a' been, I suppose, in time."

"Yes," said Massachusetts; "but before that time the Secesh himself might 'a' been counted out."

"Them fellows don't count on a game only so far as they see it," said Vermont.

"Last cherry-time was a year," said Massachusetts, "one of 'em had a deuce of a time with our fellows about a cherry-tree. She was a beauty, that tree, and just loaded with ox-hearts. Our boys was bound to have 'em, and the tree was too big to climb; but there were axes, so the boys cut her down. Goodness, how old Virginia did go on! But as every one of them fellows might be cut down themselves in half an hour, and came there for that, of course they didn't stand much for one tree more or less in Virginia."

Just then a plaintive voice broke in:

"Can any of you tell me where the Second Rhode Island Regiment is?"

They looked around, and there was another—a slim, pale fellow, who had been a good deal stouter, but was now stiff and used up with rheumatism.

"Why, she's up in front with our division. But you won't get there to-night, partner; come and sit down by the fire."

So the new-comer, saluting the Major, sat down as proposed; and in doing so brought into view a haversack whose bulging condition immediately caught the eye of Vermont.

"Got all your rations, I guess," he said.

"Yes," said Rhode Island; "I've got lots of pork and hard-tack, and no appetite. Do you want some?"

"Why," said Massachusetts, "some o' the pork would salt the pot."

"Yes," said Vermont; "and if you've got plenty of hard-tack, some of it broken up in the pot would thicken the soup."

"Well, help yourselves, boys," said Rhode Island; and he put the haversack forward between them.

Then, feeling that this reception made him perfectly at home, he got up and put his knapsack down for a seat, and disposed his rifle safely on the ground near him, and then very stiffly and painfully sat down again.

"This marching kills me," he said, "and I fell out the other day. I wish to gracious we could get the Secesh all in one corner and have it out with a square fight, so that the boys could either be comfortably buried or go home."

"Well," said Vermont, "this soup will be a great

dish, and when you get your bellyful of it you'll feel better."

"Like enough," said the other; "it smells mighty nice."

And certainly a rich fragrance more delightful than the odor of the pine-trees filled the air; and the eloquent bubble with which the juices of the old hen responded to the warm attentions of the fire made fine music for the ears of hungry men. There was now in this famous camp-kettle one hen, about four gallons of water, three or four pounds of hard bread well broken up, and a lump of salt pork half the size of a cartridge-box; while Vermont kept handy his tin cup full of a little cold water which he poured in from time to time as the boiling became two active.

"Because," he said, "if it boils too hard it will make the hen tough; and that she don't need."

Suddenly they heard a rustle of leaves, a jingle of accoutrements, and another soldier came briskly forward and stood by the fire, and broke out eloquently, as he cast his eyes about, with:

"Be my soul, b'ys, yez are having it as comfortable here as iver I saw before in the whole course of my life! I belong to the Thirty-sixth Regiment of New York Volunteers, and, by your laves, I'll be one o' the company."

They all said "Certainly," and the Irishman was immediately at home.

"And what have yez in the pot, thin, if it's a fair question?"

"Chicken soup."

"Chicken soup! Chicken soup! By the mother of Moses, did any one ever hear the loike o' that? And it's a moighty fine dish, that; a moighty fine dish is chicken soup. But, b'ys"—very seriously—"is there iver a chicken in it?"

At this they laughed boisterously.

"Well, now, b'ys, ye naydn't laugh. You know there's Massachusetts fellows and Rhode Island fellows, in our brigade, and Oi have seen them make moighty gud chicken soup wid pork and beans, and I thought it might be some of the same."

Hereupon Vermont, with two clean crotched sticks that he was using for cooking-utensils, lifted the hen into view.

"Ah, the lovely darlint!" said Pat. "Howld her there till I give her the grand salute;" and he brought his piece up in front of him, to present arms, with a ring and snap that showed his whole soul was in it. And Rhode Island, entering into the humor of the occasion, rolled the drum- with two sticks on the bottom of a tin can.

"She is a lovely craycher," said the Irishman, "and fit to lie near the hearts of hayroes."

Pat's impulse stirred them all up, and they were as musical as grasshoppers.

"But, b'ys," he said, "are there any perraties in the pot?"

There were none.

"Then bedad!" he said, "that's a great want. But you had none, I suppose. Now, I have five or six here as nice as iver came out of the ground; and though I wouldn't wrong your hospitality by an imputation that a man need pay his way among sojers, yet, if it's parliamentary, I would like to move that the perraties be put into the pot."

The motion was put by Vermont, seconded by Rhode Island, voted unanimously by Massachusetts, and the potatoes went into position on the right and left of the pork, and opposite the hen, who filled the whole danger-space in front of the line thus formed.

And then for a good while, as the soldiers prattled and smoked their pipes, and the fire crackled away, and the Major worried about the sweet little woman up the mountain, the materials in the pot bubbled themselves into soup; and at last Vermont, cooling a cup full of it nicely, set it before the Major.

And the Major, finding it of a palatable temperature, put the cup to his lips, and, tipping the bottom gradually upward, did full honor to the contents, and declared the soup was excellent; and thereupon all helped themselves and had a grand time.

Feast, feed, banquet, symposium, meal, repast, revel, high jinks, and fifty other words have been used to describe the more or less extraordinary action of swallowing, gorging, devouring, discussing, taking down, or bolting food, aliment, provender, viands, cates, rations, keep, fare, creature comforts; but not one of them does entire justice to a supper of chicken soup made by three or four old soldiers, and eaten in the Virginia woods beside a bivouac-fire. It is a refreshment that "laps over everything," as the boys said; both for the comfort it gives at the moment, and for the remembrances it revives in other days when we realize a hero's prophecy:

"—— Forsan et hæc olim meminisse juvabit."

Major Pembroke supped well on the soup and shreds of the hen; and weary with the day, and worn out with anxiety, he stretched himself on the carpet of dry pine-needles, and slept soundly, soothed to happy slumber by the crackle of the fire at his feet and the prattle of the cheery fellows about him. But the others, who could sleep at any time, enjoyed the hours about the fire in an intellectual spirit.

CHAPTER XX.

ABOUT the fire the four soldiers smoked their pipes, and in low tones of pleasant, brotherly colloquy fought their battles over again; while the Major, a little apart, fell into an uneasy sleep. In a little while the colloquy of the soldiers dwindled away to a mere fancy here and there of one or another, and then they smoked in silence; but in a true fellowship of good soldiers even silence is not dull.

Suddenly Vermont proposed that somebody should tell a story; and the proposition was hailed with the cordial surprise that might have been stirred by a great discovery.

Everybody excused himself from this duty; but finally the New-Yorker agreed to relate an account of some things that had come to his own knowledge. "It's not a story at all," he said; "but it's almost quare enough to be a story."

They accepted this as a satisfactory compromise; and he began :

"There was a gal—" And he halted as if uncertain just how to go on.

"Yes," said Massachusetts, "there's always a gal—"

"Was she handsome?" said Rhode Island.

"Handsome? Why, of course she was," said Vermont. "All gals are handsome, more or less; but anyhow there's never any stories about gals that are not handsome. But the others are sometimes very nice; and a tidy, sweet little gal is a masterpiece of nature even if her face ain't like a copper-plate picture."

"For my part," said Massachusetts, "I don't see why all stories should be about gals."

"Well, I can tell that," said Rhode Island.

"Well, what is the reason?"

"Stories are an account of the struggles and trials and hopes and victories of some fellows; and fellows are generally of a mind that there's nothing in the world worth all that—only gals."

"Well," said Pat, "who the deuce would anybody suppose was a-tellin' this story?"

"That's so," said Vermont. "Go on with the story."

"Well, there was a gal; but I'm sorry to have to inform this respectable company that she wasn't a handsome gal. She wasn't one of the kind that has eyes like stars and diamonds and things, and hair like threads of gold, and teeth like pearls, and cheeks like peaches, and lips like cherries. Oh no! Her face wasn't a fruit-stand, nor a jeweller's shop-window. She was just a quiet little girl like anybody else. Her eyes were pretty good eyes to see with; but sometimes they were dull enough to look at. And on her hair, when she wanted to cut a dash, she put the usual quantity of tricopherous and bear's grease; and when her face was yaller she put on white dust like a dabster."

"Did you ever see her do it?" said Massachusetts.

"Now, see here," said Pat: "I'm a-goin' to tell ye as much of this here story or anecdote as ye ought to know; and I don't want to be interviewed about it. See her do it? Why, for all ye know this gal was a fairy."

"No, I don't believe she was," said Vermont. "I never heard of a fairy-gal that wasn't handsome; and I guess fairies haven't got powder and bear's-grease."

"Now, even though this gal was only as handsome as other gals, she was the nicest, brightest, gayest little creature that ever chased butterflies. Her folks were pretty well off, and they lived in good style: brown-stone front, and no ash-barrels before the door. But the greatest trouble in that family was that the gal had freckles. You might imagine now that I'm travelling to get orders for a diamond, hifalutin, sure cure for freckles, only that ye know I'm a sojer. Besides, there wasn't any cure in the universe for them freckles. The family spent a fortune on it. They got poor trying to find a cure for them freckles; and at last there were the freckles all the same.

"So that interfered with the gal's chances in the matrimony-market. She wasn't handsome, I told you; but her face was bright, and she had been gay. But now the freckles spoiled the clear bright look, and she was dull too. It spoiled her temper, and made her peevish and ill-natured, and the fellows did not take to her at all; and she got unhappy, and that made it all worse; and she was just on the edge of the old-maid part of life—"

"Why, I know forty gals just like that," said Massachusetts.

"What was her name?" said Rhode Island.

"Gentlemen," said Pat, "I would have been discreet and not named any names, for family reasons; but it was Corianda.

"But to go on. Just at that most dangerous part of her life, he came—"

"Who?"

"Alonzo."

"Three cheers for Lonz!" said Vermont.

"And he fell in love with her. It may appear unreasonable. He was handsome, jovial, pleasant, and might have had any girl he wanted. He was a good mixture. He was dainty, a little, and liked to dance with the girls; but he could take things rough-and-tumble with the boys as good as any of them. He was full of good-humor and good-nature, and wherever he was it was lively. And he was the fellow that fell dead in love with Corianda. At first she didn't believe it. She thought he was fooling. It seemed impossible that he should come, as you might say, out of his element of gay and dazzling life into her dull world, to fall in love with her. But he did, and she soon understood it; and when

she understood it, it made a great difference in her.
She fell in love too; and her little soul lived in gar-
dens of delight. And the effect this pleasure had
upon her, the change it made in her soul, began to
show in her face, and she began to be handsome."

"Now that's tough to take in," said Massachusetts.

"Yes," said the Troubadour, "she grew to be
handsome. So many happy thoughts, so many
dainty impressions and delicious emotions, came
upon her, that, as all these sparkled in her eyes and
glowed in her face, they made her beautiful. You
never thought of the freckles as you looked at her;
you couldn't see them. They were dazzled out of
sight. And love, conquering all difficulties, cast
a sheen of glory about him that compelled all eyes
to rest upon that lovely little face."

"That's very pretty," said Rhode Island. "I
like a little hifalutin."

"Well, boys," said the Troubadour, "take it for
a fact that Corianda became a perfect little beauty
under the influence of a lover's eyes. Beauty
bloomed all over her, just as roses bloom in a garden when the rose-bushes feel that the summer has
come. Why it was, I don't know. Why a plain
little gal should become handsome because a fellow
falls in love is a mystery to me; but it is true, and
it's an important point in this story."

"Well, I think I know how that is," said Rhode
Island.

"Well, how?" said the Troubadour.

"Don't you know how the dogwood-leaves are in the woods, now that they're changing—what a dull dry kind of red color they have? But if you get them so that the sun shines through them, every one looks like a spot in a painted glass window, or like a glass of wine. It's the glory that comes through; and I suppose when anybody loves another person, it makes a sunshine around them and through them like that."

"Mebbe that's it," said the Troubadour; "I never thought of it that way. But Corianda became the rage with all the boys and men. Everybody courted her now, and plenty wanted to marry her, especially crowds of rich fellows. She got fearful proud of her beauty too, and the way she pushed all the other girls into the corner was a caution. She was vain and was happy.

"But of course she didn't know what it was that made her handsome. She didn't know that it was the spell of Alonzo's love; and so when the crowd came, she only counted Alonzo as one of them, and flirted with them all. Women, ye see, don't always understand the secrets of their destiny, especially when a little vanity throws dust in their eyes.

"Perhaps I didn't tell you that Alonzo wasn't very rich himself," said Pat.

"No, you didn't," said Vermont.

"But we understood it," said Massachusetts, "because we saw right away that you was Alonzo."

"Which I am not," said Pat. "This isn't any

narrative of personal experiences; and if it was, that wouldn't be fair because it would only give one side of the story, and might do injustice to the girl."

"Musn't have any injustice to the girl," said Rhode Island.

"Although Corianda was happier with Alonzo than with all the others together, she seemed not to know it; indeed the happiness that he caused her stayed with her so much that it was still with her when she was with the others, and she did not notice where it came from. Maybe you've seen one of those things they put in shop-windows which is like a bowl turned on the side with pieces of looking-glass fitted in it all around, and a candle at the bottom, so that when the bowl turns around you see that lighted candle reflected in all the little looking-glasses. There is only one real candle, but you can't tell where it is; you can hardly make out at what point burns the flame that you see reflected on every side. That was the way with Corianda's life; there was so much love all around her that she got mixed as to where the real flame was.

"Therefore, when the richest of all the crowd wanted to marry her, and her friends fixed it all up, she went through the ceremony just as if it was a dress-parade, and married old Spondulics."

"What! she married the other fellow?" said Massachusetts.

"Yes."

"She shook Lonz?" said Vermont.

"She did."

"I'm sorry," said Rhode Island; "I liked him myself. I always liked those bright fellows that make things gay. How did he take it?"

"You fellows are all too fresh," said Massachusetts. "Wait till you come to the ret-ter-ri-bew-shun."

"Yes," said the Troubadour, "there was plenty of retribution; for as soon as this happened, Alonzo was not at the party any more, and therefore Corianda's beauty began to fade; and her life was dull, and she became just as plain and common a little woman as she had been a little gal. She went out of the grand ball-room of life into the cold lonely corner where there's only a smoky lamp and the gardener's tools."

"Served her right," said Vermont; "and shows that justice is bound to be done."

"But it is a fairy-story after all," said Rhode Island. "She was rich now, though, if she wasn't handsome."

"And that's a point," said Massachusetts.

"Yes, she was rich; but she'd have given all the money to be handsome again. Her hair lost its gloss, and became so dull that even the second-hand hair men couldn't match it when she wanted a new chignon. Her teeth fell out and her cheeks fell in, and she was a woe-begone spectacle. Even old Spondulics made love to other women. But one day old Spondulics died, and when they settled up his accounts they found he was busted; didn't leave her a cent. And there she was, high and dry; no beauty, no money, and Alonzo gone."

"What did she do?" said Vermont.

"She went into the boarding-house line. Some friends of the family went security for a house and furniture to give her a start. She let out some rooms to lodgers, and had boarders in the others. It was cheap style and pretty hard hoeing, for the boarders didn't always pay. But she tried hard to keep going, and primped herself up with jet earrings; and she wore her hair with a bang and began to get fat. But she struggled on, for she had one hope. Her hope was that Alonzo would some day come that way and take board; and she intended to put him in the second-story front room for the same price for which she put other fellows in the attic; and she thought that when she should see him she'd be handsome again, and that he would love her and want to marry her, and that this time she wouldn't make any mistake; because, d'ye see, by this time, comparing how she got handsome when he came and homely when he went, she guessed at the truth of it."

And here old Thirty-six filled his pipe, as if he were near the end.

"Well, did he come?" said Vermont.

"He didn't," said Pat. "Her preparations was no use at all."

"Why didn't he?" sympathetically queried Little Rhody.

"Because there wasn't any more any Alonzo."

16

This tragic declaration caused a great sensation; and the New-Yorker, seeing the great impatience of the others, went on swiftly with the story.

"Ye see, as soon as Alonzo saw how things was going he went out and bought five pounds of nitroglycerine, which explodes tremendously, you know. He had an apothecary mix it with something till it was just like soft grease. Then he got a paint-brush and painted himself all over with it; and he put on his clothes very softly for fear he might explode too soon, and went out.

"He'd often been bothered by those fellows that sits in the horse-cars with their feet poked out and don't make room for any one, and laugh if you stumble over them, and tell you that your feet is too big. He thought he'd fix some of 'em. So he got into a horse-car. But everybody was as smooth as old potheen; and they made way for him as perlite as if they know'd what he was up to.

"But he sat down quietly, 'For,' says he to himself, 'somebody'll come in with a couple of kegs of paint in a minute and he'll slap 'em down on my knees, and then the fun will begin;' and he laughed a little jolly laugh as he thought about it."

"He was gone mad," said Rhode Island.

"But no painter was around that day, and there didn't come into that car not even an old washerwoman with a bundle of dirty clothes."

"Life is full of such disappointments," said Massachusetts, who was ready to rejoice in the explosion.

"So Alonzo got out of the car in disgust, and went to the ferry, where everybody almost knocks you down to get on the boat first; but everybody was cool and slow and went easy that time. Seemed as if he couldn't get no brutal treatment anywhere.

"Just as he was thinking of this, he saw a cop on the other side of the street. 'Pleeceman's the racket,' he said; 'pleeceman's sure for brutality every time.' So he watched the pleeceman, and saw two or three of them get around a gin-mill at the corner and buzz. He went into that gin-mill and had some gin and sugar, and put five cents down on the bar, softly like. But the bar-tender said, 'Come, Johnny, that wasn't no five-cent gin.' Then he give the bar-tender a little jaw, and that fellow ran around the end of the bar and called the cops, and said there was a fellow there that wanted to murder him.

"Then the cops all rushed in with their clubs ready, and the bar-tender caught Alonzo by the collar, and every one was getting a hold of him somewhere, and a-pulling and a-hauling, and Alonzo was a-laughing softly, enjoying himself.

"But there was one pleeceman that couldn't find no place to get hold; and he hauled off with his club and give Alonzo one on the head.

"Well, that fetched it! Alonzo, ye see, had put the stuff very thick in his hair. That fetched it. He went off with an awful report. And them cops, and the bar-tender, and the whole place was smashed to smithereens. They was smashed so fine that they even beat the coroner, because they couldn't pick up enough of them for the coroner to sit on ; and therefore there wasn't any inquest.

"And that," said old Thirty-six, solemnly, " is the end of the history of Alonzo and Corianda."

And the boys all laughed about it, and critically discussed the various points, and held that it " had the bulge" on the Arabian Nights.

CHAPTER XXI.

THE ROAR OF BATTLE.

SOME of the fellows were on foot from time to time all through the night and fed the fire; so that when Vermont went at it in the gray and foggy dawn to get ready for an early start, there was a blaze in no time; and as the persistent activity of one moved all, there were soon four cups on the fire, and coffee was made, and they had a comfortable breakfast.

They had scarcely got through with this when they were all brought to their feet by a sudden tremendous outburst of firing, so near and so loud that it seemed all around them.

Now, the sound that thus disturbed our friends about the bivouac-fire was that historic noise, "the roar of battle;" and as the reader may never have heard that noise, and as it is often mentioned but seldom described, it may not be unprofitable to endeavor to give an impression of its nature and peculiarities.

Battle, let it be understood, roars, not with one vocal organ, but with many organs, or indeed with many thousand organs. It has more carnivorous throats than all the jungles in India. There may be a hundred thousand rifles, each one of which alone has a peremptory voice, trivial enough in itself; but when these staccato tones follow so rapidly that they are blended as drops of water in the noise of the rain, the muzzles that deliver them become practically innumerable. And there may be the mouths of five hundred cannon; and the mouths of frantic horses, torn to ribbons with shot and shell; and the mouths of bugles that stir the blood of the fellows who are there, and of the fellows who are coming up. And there are many mouths of men as the line of battle advances, or as the boys are sent to storm the hill and get the enemy's battery.

Therefore the roar of battle is an agglomeration of various noises mingled at different times in different proportions.

But the natural order of the noises is this:

Perhaps during the day an occasional spurt of cannonading has wakened the far-away echoes, as the first muttering thunder does an hour before the storm; and then there is perhaps an hour or two or three of silence, and suddenly away at the front is heard—one rifle-shot! And then another rifle-shot! Another and another! And then rifle-shots follow as if they ran up and down a gamut: tap, tap, tap—slip, slap—bang—rattlety-crack! And so until from a dropping fire of one or two shots in a second it increases until it becomes nearly continuous, but keeps light—as the drops of a summer shower that patter on the green leaves, rather than as the pounding flood of the autumn storm that comes upon the house-top. It is like the first tremulous venture of the voice trying its scales, or like the tuning up that comes before the concert.

Now, this noise means that the pickets away out in front, or on one of the flanks, have seen the enemy, and that the enemy is behaving himself in a way that needs attention; that he is coming on in line through the woods or across the plain, or is getting the abatis out of the way.

Then there is a bugle-call, clear and high, and the fire ceases.

Major Thundereye, in command of the main guard on that part of the front, has jumped to his feet at the first shot, and from his coign of vantage has taken a cool look at the enemy, and has seen that the enemy means it; has made out that the dirty gray line of infantry stretches away to his left and right; that it is an advance in force; that the big dirty pocket-handkerchiefs with diagonal crosses on them which the enemy calls battle-flags are in the air, and that it is no use for him to waste time with his boys on the first line.

Hence his bugle-note orders them to retire upon their supports; and at the same instant an orderly dashes away rearward from that post to tell Thundereye's commanding officer in the rear what Thundereye has seen.

But the respite will be short, for the pickets have not far to go, and the enemy comes on.

And now there is a rapid firing of cannon far away in front, and a screaming of shells in the air, and a bursting of shells behind our line; for the enemy, learning by our fire that his movement is observed, comprehends that there is no surprise in it, and begins to shell our position in the hope to distract our attention and so help the advance of his infantry.   At the same moment one of our batteries far away to the left sights the enemy's line as it reaches a clear point, and opens upon it; and this mutual attention, and the noisy flight of shells and their explosion just over one's head, keep things from becoming altogether dull.

But now the enemy is up to where he is fairly under fire from Major Thundereye's line, which is well advanced beyond the point at which the general means to fight, and word has been sent to Thundereye to hold the enemy a little and give a chance to get the whole force in shape.

Thundereye does what he can, and the air vibrates with the close rattle of a steady file-fire—a sound that snaps and seems about to stop, but goes on; that tears away for ten minutes, and stops the enemy and then tears away again, and at last ceases altogether.

Thundereye finds that he has done all he can, and comes in slowly.

And now there is a real intermission.   Our considerate enemy is taking a long look at us.   In front of Thundereye he has reached a point at which his serious attempt begins.   Down to his left or to his right they had not advanced so far.   He must wait till they get up even and complete his line; and he waits. And we all wait; and some of the boys even make a cup of coffee.

Fellows in the reserve begin to wonder whether it was not a false alarm; whether the enemy had not simply made a reconnoissance in force to see just where we are, and is not now getting away again.

"It's all over," says one teamster to another.

"No, 'tain't, pardner," says the other; "it's too still."

And just as these doubts are floating in men's minds, the canopy of heaven seems to be rent asunder with the roar that suddenly arises, for the enemy has started forward, and a very little movement has brought him into the field of fire of all our batteries placed to dispute his advance; they have all got the range, and they all open. "Cannon to right of them, cannon to left of them;" cannon over the hill, cannon on the other side the river, cannon down the road, cannon hidden in the woods and firing over the roof of the stone house yonder; and twenty or thirty cannon blazing right in their faces with grape and canister; cannon so near that they fancy they can touch them—though when they get where they would touch them, the few that are left of the line find it may be twenty yards of an impassable morass between.

And all the cannon are banging away at once, so that it is a nearly continuous sound; and the air vibrates with the ring of the brass and the steel, and you cannot tell whether the shell that bursts within

a yard of your head is not another cannon coming
into action in front of you or down the road. Altogether it is a glorious row.

But all this that is merely the voice of cannon
you have heard before: you may hear it often
enough in the salvoes of days of glorification in
times of peace, though perhaps rather less of it at
once. There is another noise peculiar to battle, that
you do not hear except in battle—a strange, startling,
unearthly note. This is the flight of a shell through
the air. It is one of the odd contradictions of
speech that though we say the shell flies, yet if one
is particularly noisy it is on account of a bad shoe.
Any shell makes noise enough, and the passage
of one through the air affects the unaccustomed
thought with consternation; yet there is a constant
tone and a harmony in it while the shoe is right.
The shoe is that band of lead or other soft metal
that enables the shell to take the grooves of the
cannon; and when that is half torn off, the eccen-
tric way in which it cuts the air gives to the voice
of this bird of battle some altogether horrible variations.

But the most carnivorous note has yet to come.

There were twenty or thirty cannon blazing in the
very faces of the enemy, who, as we said, thought
they could touch them, and suddenly found an impassable morass between. Well, the morass was
not impassable. The enemy's line with bayonets
fixed rushed fair at the guns: and the brigade in
front of the guns just melted away in the fire.

Half of them are dead or dying in the morass; two or three score are stuck there and can get neither one way nor the other, and about a hundred have struggled through and are lying flat on their faces on our side the wet ground, almost under the muzzles of the guns, but hidden by the heavy screen of dense white smoke that is accumulated in front of the pieces.

And now a part of the enemy's line that was not in front of the guns have got through the bad ground more successfully, and, wheeling to right and left respectively, are charging down upon the pieces, while the fellows there under the muzzles are lying ready to jump up and take a hand in at the right moment.

In such a case the battery is helpless if it is alone. But behold! it is not alone. Lying down at just a handy distance behind it are two fresh regiments of our own infantry, placed there to support the guns; and as the rebs rush upon the guns with a yell of triumph, their yell is turned to the demoniac wail of defeat and death, for the regiments are up and pouring into the heap of the enemy their close file-fire.

This gives that rapid, close-packed, continuous sound that is the real familiar, personal voice of the god of war—the sound that soothes the souls of heroes to the eternal sleep; the real death-rattle of hostile armies.

With an empty barrel and some packs of squibs one may mimic this sound about as it is heard a mile away; but if a fellow wants to know how it sounds when it is fired fair in his face, he must go and listen. Nobody can tell him.

But the rebs' attempt at the guns is pretty well dusted up by the file-fire, yet they keep coming; and the fellows that lay down awhile in front of the pieces are among the guns, and the battery-men are fighting with clubbed rammers. Then a bugle-note sounds "Cease firing," the word passes "Fix bayonets," there is a musical jingle of blue steel against steel up and down the line with a suppressed cheer, and in another instant away goes the line, and the rebel attempt in that part of the battle disappears as the tall stems in the cornfield go down where the cyclone strikes. One cannot tell whether it was the bayonets or the hurrah that did it. Generally it is the hurrah; but the hurrah wouldn't count if those who hear it did not know that the bayonets were there.

Now, these are the separate elements of the roar of battle; and their parts follow, not in an ordinary sequence, but as the parts follow in a fugue, each adding its own notes to the already-gathered-up accumulation of other notes. And when this row tears up through the tranquil atmosphere, the shivered air seems alive to a conscious horror; the sun trembles in the heavens; the hushed winds scoot quietly away down the remote gulches; the women and the old men in the villages near gather up their little ones and fly, and the soldiers on the march shut their mouths and go forward as if there were no time to be lost in gabble.

Our friends did not hear on this occasion what may be called the prelude to the grand roar, because there was none. This battle broke into a full diapason, as if it began in the middle: which in fact it did. And we shall now see how that came about.

UPON A CAST.

A Novel. By CHARLOTTE DUNNING. pp. 330. 16mo, Cloth, $1 00.

It embodies throughout the expressions of genuine American frankness, is well conceived, well managed, and brought to a delightful and captivating close.—*Albany Press.*

The author writes this story of American social life in an interesting manner. . . . The style of the writing is excellent, and the dialogue clever.—*N. Y. Times.*

This story is strong in plot, and its characters are drawn with a firm and skilful hand. They seem like real people, and their acts and words, their fortunes and misadventures, are made to engage the reader's interest and sympathy.—*Worcester Daily Spy.*

The character painting is very well done. . . . The sourest cynic that ever sneered at woman cannot but find the little story vastly entertaining.—*Commercial Bulletin*, Boston.

The life of a semi-metropolitan village, with its own aristocracy, gossips, and various other qualities of people, is admirably portrayed. . . . The book fascinates the reader from the first page to the last.—*Boston Traveller.*

The plot has been constructed with no little skill, and the characters—all of them interesting and worthy of acquaintance—are portrayed with great distinctness. The book is written in an entertaining and vivacious style, and is destined to provide entertainment for a large number of readers.—*Christian at Work*, N. Y.

One of the best—if not the very best—of the society novels of the season.—*Detroit Free Press.*

Of peculiar interest as regards plot, and with much grace and freshness of style.—*Brooklyn Times.*

The plot has been constructed with no little skill, and the characters —all of them interesting and worthy of acquaintance—are portrayed with great distinctness.—*Episcopal Recorder*, Philadelphia.

A clever and entertaining novel. It is wholly social, and the theatre is a small one; but the characters are varied and are drawn with a firm hand; the play of human passion and longing is well-defined and brilliant; and the movement is effective and satisfactory. . . . The love story is as good as the social study, making altogether an uncommonly entertaining book for vacation reading.—*Wilmington* (Del.) *Morning News.*

PUBLISHED BY HARPER & BROTHERS, NEW YORK.

☞ HARPER & BROTHERS *will send the above work by mail, postage prepaid, to any part of the United States or Canada, on receipt of the price.*

GEORGE ELIOT'S LIFE AND WORKS.

LIBRARY EDITION.

14 vols., 12mo, Cloth, $1 25 per vol.   Complete Sets, $15 75.

ADAM BEDE. Illustrated.

DANIEL DERONDA. 2 vols.

ESSAYS AND LEAVES FROM A NOTE-BOOK.

FELIX HOLT, THE RADICAL. Illustrated.

GEORGE ELIOT'S LIFE. By J. W. Cross. With Portraits and Illustrations. 3 vols.

MIDDLEMARCH. 2 vols.

ROMOLA. Illustrated.

SCENES OF CLERICAL LIFE, and SILAS MARNER. Illustrated.

THE IMPRESSIONS OF THEO-PHRASTUS SUCH.

THE MILL ON THE FLOSS. Illustrated.

POPULAR EDITION.

11 vols., 12mo, Cloth, 75 cents per vol.

ADAM BEDE. Illustrated.

DANIEL DERONDA. 2 vols.

ESSAYS AND LEAVES FROM A NOTE-BOOK.

FELIX HOLT, THE RADICAL. Illustrated.

MIDDLEMARCH. 2 vols.

ROMOLA. Illustrated.

SCENES OF CLERICAL LIFE, and SILAS MARNER. Illustrated.

THE IMPRESSIONS OF THEO-PHRASTUS SUCH.

THE MILL ON THE FLOSS. Illustrated.

PAPER EDITION.

BROTHER JACOB.—THE LIFTED VEIL. 32mo, 20 cents.

DANIEL DERONDA. 8vo, 50 cents.

FELIX HOLT. 8vo, 50 cents.

GEORGE ELIOT'S LIFE. By J. W. Cross. With Three Illustrations. 3 vols., 4to, 15 cents each.

MIDDLEMARCH. 8vo, 75 cents.

ROMOLA. Illustrated. 8vo, 50 cents.

SCENES OF CLERICAL LIFE. 8vo, 50 cents. Separately, in 32mo: *The Sad Fortunes of the Rev. Amos Barton*, 20 cents; *Mr. Gilfil's Love Story*, 20 cents; *Janet's Repentance*, 20 cents.

SILAS MARNER. 12mo, 20 cents.

THE IMPRESSIONS OF THEOPHRASTUS SUCH. 4to, 10 cents.

THE MILL ON THE FLOSS. 8vo, 50 cents.

PUBLISHED BY HARPER & BROTHERS, NEW YORK.

☞ HARPER & BROTHERS *will send any of the above works by mail, postage prepaid, to any part of the United States or Canada, on receipt of the price.*

MISS MULOCK'S WORKS.

LIBRARY EDITION.

Illustrated. 12mo, Cloth, 90 cents per vol. Complete Sets (25 vols.), $22 50; Half Calf, $60 00.

A BRAVE LADY.
A HERO.
A LEGACY.
A LIFE FOR A LIFE.
A NOBLE LIFE.
AGATHA'S HUSBAND.
CHRISTIAN'S MISTAKE.
HANNAH.
HEAD OF THE FAMILY.
HIS LITTLE MOTHER, &c.
JOHN HALIFAX.
MISS TOMMY.
MISTRESS AND MAID.

MY MOTHER AND I.
OGILVIES.
OLIVE.
PLAIN-SPEAKING.
SERMONS OUT OF CHURCH.
STUDIES FROM LIFE.
THE FAIRY BOOK.
THE LAUREL BUSH.
TWO MARRIAGES.
UNKIND WORD, &c.
WOMAN'S KINGDOM.
YOUNG MRS. JARDINE.

PAPER EDITION.

A BRAVE LADY. Ill'd. 8vo, 60 cents.
A LIFE FOR A LIFE. 8vo, 40 cents.
AGATHA'S HUSBAND. 8vo, 35 cents.
AVILLION, AND OTHER TALES. 8vo, 60 cts.
HANNAH. Illustrated. 8vo, 35 cents.
HIS LITTLE MOTHER, &c. 4to, 10 cents.
JOHN HALIFAX, GENTLEMAN. 8vo, 50 cents; 4to, 15 cents.
MISS TOMMY. Ill'd. 12mo, 50 cents.
MISTRESS AND MAID. 8vo, 30 cents.
NOTHING NEW. 8vo, 30 cents.

MY MOTHER AND I. Illustrated. 8vo, 40 cents.
OGILVIES. 8vo, 35 cents.
OLIVE. 8vo, 35 cents.
PLAIN-SPEAKING. 4to, 15 cents.
THE HEAD OF THE FAMILY. 8vo, 50 cents.
THE LAUREL BUSH. Ill'd. 8vo, 25 cts.
THE WOMAN'S KINGDOM. Illustrated. 8vo, 60 cents.
YOUNG MRS. JARDINE. 4to, 10 cents.

JUVENILES.

A FRENCH COUNTRY FAMILY. Illustrated. 12mo, Cloth, $1 50.
BOOKS FOR GIRLS. Written or Edited by Miss MULOCK. Illustrated. 16mo, Cloth, 90 cents each.

> AN ONLY SISTER.—IS IT TRUE?—LITTLE SUNSHINE'S HOLIDAY.—MISS MOORE.—THE COUSIN FROM INDIA.—TWENTY YEARS AGO.

MOTHERLESS; OR, A PARISIAN FAMILY. Illustrated. 12mo, Cloth, $1 50.
OUR YEAR. Illustrated. 16mo, Cloth, $1 00.
THE ADVENTURES OF A BROWNIE. Illustrated. Square 16mo, Cloth, 90 cts.
THE LITTLE LAME PRINCE AND HIS TRAVELLING CLOAK. Ill'd. Square 16mo, Cloth, $1 00.

MISCELLANEOUS.

SONGS OF OUR YOUTH. Set to Music. Square 4to, Cloth, $2 50.
FAIR FRANCE. Impressions of a Traveller. 12mo, Cloth, $1 50.

PUBLISHED BY HARPER & BROTHERS, NEW YORK.

☞ HARPER & BROTHERS *will send any of the above works by mail, postage prepaid, to any part of the United States or Canada, on receipt of the price.*

CHARLES READE'S WORKS.

LIBRARY EDITION.

Illustrated. 12mo, Cloth, $1 00 per vol. Complete Sets, 14 vols., Cloth, $12 00; Half Calf, $36 00.

A SIMPLETON, AND THE WANDERING HEIR.
A TERRIBLE TEMPTATION.
A WOMAN-HATER.
FOUL PLAY.
GOOD STORIES.
GRIFFITH GAUNT.
HARD CASH.

IT IS NEVER TOO LATE TO MEND.
LOVE ME LITTLE, LOVE ME LONG.
PEG WOFFINGTON, &c.
PUT YOURSELF IN HIS PLACE.
THE CLOISTER AND THE HEARTH.
WHITE LIES.

A PERILOUS SECRET. 12mo, Cloth, 75 cents.

PAPER EDITION.

A HERO AND A MARTYR. With a Portrait. 8vo, 15 cents.

A PERILOUS SECRET. 12mo, 40 cents; 4to, 20 cents.

A SIMPLETON. 8vo, 30 cents.

A TERRIBLE TEMPTATION. Illustrated. 8vo, 25 cents.

A WOMAN-HATER. Illustrated. 8vo, 30 cents; 12mo, 20 cents.

FOUL PLAY. 8vo, 30 cents.

GOOD STORIES OF MAN AND OTHER ANIMALS. Illustrated. 12mo, 50 cents; 4to, 20 cents.

GRIFFITH GAUNT. Illustrated. 8vo, 30 cents.

HARD CASH. Illustrated. 8vo, 35 cents.

IT IS NEVER TOO LATE TO MEND. 8vo, 35 cents.

JACK OF ALL TRADES. 16mo, 15 cents.

LOVE ME LITTLE, LOVE ME LONG. 8vo, 30 cents.

MULTUM IN PARVO. Illustrated. 4to, 15 cents.

PEG WOFFINGTON, CHRISTIE JOHNSTONE, AND OTHER TALES. 8vo, 35 cents.

PUT YOURSELF IN HIS PLACE. Illustrated. 8vo, 35 cents.

THE CLOISTER AND THE HEARTH. 8vo, 35 cents.

THE COMING MAN. 32mo, 20 cents.

THE JILT. Illustrated. 32mo, 20 cents.

THE PICTURE. 16mo, 15 cents.

THE WANDERING HEIR. Illustrated. 8vo, 20 cents.

WHITE LIES. 8vo, 30 cents.

PUBLISHED BY HARPER & BROTHERS, NEW YORK.

☞ HARPER & BROTHERS *will send any of the above works by mail, postage prepaid, to any part of the United States or Canada, on receipt of the price.*

WILLIAM BLACK'S NOVELS.

LIBRARY EDITION.

12mo, Cloth, $1 25 per vol. Complete Sets, 15 vols., $17 50; Half Calf, $34 75.

A DAUGHTER OF HETH.

A PRINCESS OF THULE.

GREEN PASTURES AND PICCA-DILLY.

IN SILK ATTIRE.

JUDITH SHAKESPEARE. Ill'd.

KILMENY.

MACLEOD OF DARE. Illustrated.

MADCAP VIOLET.

SHANDON BELLS. Illustrated.

STRANGE ADVENTURES OF A PHAETON.

SUNRISE.

THAT BEAUTIFUL WRETCH. Illustrated.

THREE FEATHERS.

WHITE WINGS. Illustrated.

YOLANDE. Illustrated.

PAPER EDITION.

A DAUGHTER OF HETH. 8vo, 35 cents.

A PRINCESS OF THULE. 8vo, 50 cents.

AN ADVENTURE IN THULE. 4to, 10 cents.

GREEN PASTURES AND PICCADILLY. 8vo, 50 cents.

IN SILK ATTIRE. 8vo, 35 cents.

JUDITH SHAKESPEARE. 4to, 20 cents.

KILMENY. 8vo, 35 cents.

MACLEOD OF DARE. 8vo, Illustrated, 60 cents; 4to, 15 cents.

MADCAP VIOLET. 8vo, 50 cents.

SHANDON BELLS. Illustrated. 4to, 20 cents.

STRANGE ADVENTURES OF A PHAETON. 8vo, 50 cents.

SUNRISE. 4to, 15 cents.

THAT BEAUTIFUL WRETCH. Illustrated. 4to, 20 cents.

THE MAID OF KILLEENA, THE MARRIAGE OF MOIRA FERGUS, and other Stories. 8vo, 40 cents.

THE MONARCH OF MINCING-LANE. Illustrated. 8vo, 50 cents.

THREE FEATHERS. Illustrated. 8vo, 50 cents.

WHITE WINGS. 4to, 20 cents.

YOLANDE. Illustrated. 4to, 20 cents.

PUBLISHED BY HARPER & BROTHERS, NEW YORK.

☞ HARPER & BROTHERS *will send any of the above works by mail, postage prepaid, to any part of the United States or Canada, on receipt of the price.*

BOOTS AND SADDLES;

Or, Life in Dakota with General Custer. By Mrs. ELIZ-
ABETH B. CUSTER. With Portrait of General Custer.
pp. 312. 12mo, Cloth, $1 50.

A book of adventure is interesting reading, especially when it is all true,
as is the case with "Boots and Saddles." * * * She does not obtrude the
fact that sunshine and solace went with her to tent and fort, but it in-
heres in her narrative none the less, and as a consequence "these simple
annals of our daily life," as she calls them, are never dull nor uninterest-
ing.—*Evangelist*, N. Y.

Mrs. Custer's book is in reality a bright and sunny sketch of the life
of her late husband, who fell at the battle of "Little Big Horn." * * *
After the war, when General Custer was sent to the Indian frontier, his
wife was of the party, and she is able to give the minute story of her
husband's varied career, since she was almost always near the scene of
his adventures.—*Brooklyn Union*.

We have no hesitation in saying that no better or more satisfactory life
of General Custer could have been written. Indeed, we may as well
speak the thought that is in us, and say plainly that we know of no bio-
graphical work anywhere which we count better than this. * * * Surely the
record of such experiences as these will be read with that keen interest
which attaches only to strenuous human doings; as surely we are right
in saying that such a story of truth and heroism as that here told will
take a deeper hold upon the popular mind and heart than any work of
fiction can. For the rest, the narrative is as vivacious and as lightly and
trippingly given as that of any novel. It is enriched in every chapter with
illustrative anecdotes and incidents, and here and there a little life story
of pathetic interest is told as an episode.—*N. Y. Commercial Advertiser*.

It is a plain, straightforward story of the author's life on the plains of
Dakota. Every member of a Western garrison will want to read this
book; every person in the East who is interested in Western life will
want to read it, too; and every girl or boy who has a healthy appetite
for adventure will be sure to get it. It is bound to have an army of readers that few authors can expect.—*Philadelphia Press*.

These annals of daily life in the army are simple, yet interesting, and
underneath all is discerned the love of a true woman ready for any sacrifice. She touches on themes little canvassed by the civilian, and makes a
volume equally redolent of a loving devotion to an honored husband, and
attractive as a picture of necessary duty by the soldier.—*Commonwealth*,
Boston.

PUBLISHED BY HARPER & BROTHERS, N. Y.

☞ HARPER & BROTHERS *will send the above work by mail, postage prepaid, to any
part of the United States or Canada, on receipt of the price.*

CHARLES NORDHOFF'S WORKS.

POLITICS FOR YOUNG AMERICANS. By CHARLES NORDHOFF. 16mo, Half Leather, 75 cents; Paper, 40 cents.

It is a book that should be in the hand of every American boy and girl. This book of Mr. Nordhoff's might be learned by heart. Each word has its value; each enumerated section has its pith. It is a complete system of political science, economical and other, as applied to our American system.—*N. Y. Herald.*

CALIFORNIA: A Book for Travellers and Settlers. By CHARLES NORDHOFF. A New Edition. With Maps and Illustrations. 8vo, Cloth, $2 00.

Mr. Nordhoff's plan is to see what is curious, important, and true, and then to tell it in the simplest manner. Herodotus is evidently his prototype. Strong sense, a Doric truthfulness, and a very earnest contempt for anything like pretension or sensationalism, and an enthusiasm none the less agreeable because straitened in its expression, are his qualities.—*N. Y. Evening Post.*

THE COMMUNISTIC SOCIETIES OF THE UNITED STATES; from Personal Visit and Observation: including Detailed Accounts of the Economists, Zoarites, Shakers; the Amana, Oneida, Bethel, Aurora, Icarian, and other Existing Societies; their Religious Creeds, Social Practices, Numbers, Industries, and Present Condition. By CHARLES NORDHOFF. Illustrated. 8vo, Cloth, $4 00.

Mr. Nordhoff has derived his materials from personal observation, having visited the principal Communistic societies in the United States, and taken diligent note of the peculiar features of their religious creed and practices, their social and domestic customs, and their industrial and financial arrangements. * * * With his exceptionally keen powers of perception, and his habits of practised observation, he could not engage in such an inquiry without amassing a fund of curious information. In stating the results of his investigations, he writes with exemplary candor and impartiality, though not without the exercise of just and sound discrimination.—*N. Y. Tribune.*

CAPE COD AND ALL ALONG SHORE: STORIES. By CHARLES NORDHOFF. 12mo, Cloth, $1 50; 4to, Paper, 15 cents.

Light, clever, well-written sketches.—*N. Y. Times.*
A lively and agreeable volume, full of humor and incident.—*Boston Transcript.*

GOD AND THE FUTURE LIFE. The Reasonableness of Christianity. By CHARLES NORDHOFF. 16mo, Cloth, $1 00.

Mr. Nordhoff's object is not so much to present a religious system as to give practical and sufficient reasons for every-day beliefs. He writes strongly, clearly, and in the vein that the people understand.—*Boston Herald.*

PUBLISHED BY HARPER & BROTHERS, NEW YORK.

☞ HARPER & BROTHERS *will send the above works by mail, postage prepaid, to any part of the United States or Canada, on receipt of the price.*

OATS OR WILD OATS?

Common-sense for Young Men. By J. M. BUCKLEY, LL.D.
pp. xiv., 306. 12mo, Cloth, $1 50.

It is a good book, which ought to do good on a large scale. . . . Such passages as those headed Tact, Observation, Reflection, Self-command, and the like, may be read and re-read many times with advantage.—*Brooklyn Union.*

A book which should be recommended to the consideration of every young man who is preparing to go into a business career or any other in which he may aspire to become an honorable, useful, and prosperous citizen. . . . Dr. Buckley knows the trials and the temptations to which young men are exposed, and his book, while written in most agreeable language, is full of excellent counsel, and illustrations are given by anecdotes and by examples which the author has observed or heard of in his own experience. Besides general advice, there are especial chapters relating to professional, commercial, and other occupations. So good a book should be widely distributed, and it will tell on the next generation.—*Philadelphia Bulletin.*

It is a model manual, and will be as interesting to a bright, go-ahead boy as a novel.—*Philadelphia Record.*

The scheme of the book is to assist young men in the choice of a profession or life pursuit by explaining the leading principles and characteristics of different branches of business, so that the reader may see what his experiences are likely to be, and thus be enabled to make an intelligent selection among the many avenues of labor. In order to make his work accurate and comprehensive, Dr. Buckley has consulted merchants, lawyers, statesmen, farmers, manufacturers, men in all walks of life, and specialists of every description, visiting and examining their establishments, offices, and studios. From the knowledge thus gained he has prepared the greater part of his book The remainder is given to general advice, and contains the old maxims familiar to all young men from the time of Poor Richard. Success is won by good behavior, intelligence, and industry. These are the "Oats." The "Wild Oats" of laziness, carelessness, and dissipation bring ruin, disaster, and misery. The work is likely to attract readers from its practical value as a compendium of facts relating to the various departments of labor rather than on account of its moral injunctions. It cannot help being very useful to the class of young men for whom it is intended, as also to parents who have boys to start out into the world.—*N. Y. Times.*

PUBLISHED BY HARPER & BROTHERS, NEW YORK.

☞ HARPER & BROTHERS *will send the above work by mail, postage prepaid. to any part of the United States or Canada, on receipt of the price.*

AMERICAN POLITICAL IDEAS,

Viewed from the Standpoint of Universal History. By JOHN
FISKE. pp. 158. 12mo, Cloth, $1 00.

Mr. Fiske is one of the few Americans who is able to exercise
a dispassionate judgment upon questions which have been the
cause of quarrels between parties and sections. Mr. Fiske has a
calm way of considering our modern ideas from the standpoint
of universal history.—*N. Y. Journal of Commerce.*

We know of no treatise concerning American history which is
likely to exercise larger or better influence in leading Americans to
read between the lines of our country's annals. * * * The little
book is so direct and simple in the manner of its presentation of
truth, so attractive in substance, that its circulation is likely to
be wide. Its appeal is as directly to the farmer or mechanic as
to the philosophic student of politics or history.—*N. Y. Commercial
Advertiser.*

There is not a line in the entire work which is not laden with
the richest fruits of a trained and powerful intellect.—*Commercial
Bulletin,* Boston.

When Mr. Fiske comes to discuss American history by the comparative method, he enters a field of special and vital interest to
all who have ever taken up this method of study. Our history, as
the author says, when viewed in this broad and yet impartial way,
acquires a new dignity. There is no need to say that Mr. Fiske's
pages are worthy of the most careful study.—*Brooklyn Union.*

From this point of view the consideration of the political ideas
of this country becomes something more than a mere study of
history; it constitutes a page of philosophy, a social study of the
most transcendant importance. Such is the spirit with which
Prof. Fiske handles his subject. He shows how our institutions
have grown and developed from the past, how they have a firm
basis in nature, and how they must develop in the future. The
lectures are important reading; they are also pleasant reading, for
the literary style of Prof. Fiske is exceptionally pure, clear, and
graceful.—*Boston Gazette.*

A volume of great interest, and illustrates very happily some of
the fundamental ideas of American politics by setting forth their
relations to the general history of mankind. * * * We heartily
commend this little volume to such of our readers as desire to en-
large their ideas and views of the political principles underlying the
foundations of our system of government.—*Christian at Work,* N. Y.

PUBLISHED BY HARPER & BROTHERS, NEW YORK.

www.ingramcontent.com/pod-product-compliance
Lightning Source LLC
Chambersburg PA
CBHW030642030726
47497CB00006B/1905